Through My Picture Window

My Picture Window

Peering out my window at break of day,
I behold the fragrant lilacs, trembling in the wind.
Just below, the hill drops sharply to the peaceful valley
And quaint little village below.
In the distance loom the mighty Blacks,
Tall and majestic:
Clingman's Peak, Le Conte, Mt. Mitchell—The Grand
    Dame of them all—
Her tower pointing upward,
Like a slender arrow
Shimmering in the sunlight,
Poised restlessly, awaiting the Mighty Arm to loose its
    bow,
Its dark rolling mounds of earth—
Eternal as any earthly thing can be.

— R.B. Phillips

THROUGH
MY
PICTURE WINDOW

by
Robert B. Phillips
(author of "One of God's Children")

Observations on learning, living, and loving. Written and compiled by an 85-year-old North Carolina mountain man who grew up in the shadow of Mt. Mitchell.

Illustrated with photographs of sculpture in Brookgreen Gardens, Murrell's Inlet, South Carolina.

Bakersville, North Carolina
1988

Copies of this book may be obtained from selected dealers or ·
from the author: Robert B. Phillips, 175 Slagle Road, Bakersville NC 28705. (704) 688–4850.

Produced through Celo Press Production Services, 1901 Han-
nah Branch Road, Burnsville NC 28714.

ISBN 0-9620577-1-1
Library of Congress Catalog Card Number 88-90649

TABLE OF CONTENTS

Youth and Age 1
Education 25
Music 41
Nature 47
Character 61
Work 75
Motherhood 89
Moral Crisis 99
Wealth and Poverty 115
Courage 133
Suffering and Death 143
Despair 173
Comfort 181
Forgiveness and Mercy 193
Happiness 203
Love 221
Immortality 237

v

PREFACE

"To say that I'm a self-made man," said Speaker of the House James Wright, Jr., "relieves the Almighty of a terrible responsibility."

Indeed, there are no self-made men. Throughout our lives, we make a part of ourselves all the people we have met, whether personally or through literature. In this little book I have carefully collected choice writings that have brought me joy and enlightenment during my eighty-five years. Included are many pieces gleaned from my reading and stored in my files for half a century. A few of my own creative writing efforts have also been added.

Wherever I could, I have acknowledged the authors. I beg indulgence from those to whom I have not been able to give credit. I am of course grateful to all of them, as all have contributed to making my own life meaningful and worthwhile. I feel confident that the writers I have quoted would be pleased to know that I am attempting to pass on a part of their lives for the pleasure and enlightenment of future generations.

— *R.B. Phillips*

This book is dedicated to my many friends who have expressed their joy in reading my first book, *One of God's Children*.

———·◆·◆·◆·——

Shakespeare was of us, Milton was for us, Burns, Shelley, were with us. They watch from their graves!

— *Robert Browning*

Between Yesterday and Tomorrow, Edith Howland.
Courtesy of Brookgreen Gardens.

> I move like a prisoner caught
> From behind me comes my shadow,
> And before me goes my thought.
> — *from base of statue*

YOUTH AND AGE

Yesterday, today, and tomorrow—each has its own pain and suffering, and also its own joys and delights.

In infancy all our needs had to be met and decisions made. We had no choice. At sixteen we may have doubted the judgment of anybody older than thirty. If we wanted information we talked to Big Harry Jowaski—he was captain of the football team and generally knew all the answers. As we grew older we should have become wiser and humbler.

———◆◆◆———

. . . Old age hath yet his honor and his toil.
Death closes all. But something ere the end,
Some work of noble note may yet be done,
Not unbecoming men that strove with Gods.
. . . To strive, to seek, to find, and not to yield.
— *Alfred Lord Tennyson, (Ulysses)*

———◆◆◆———

1

What a Man!

Some fellows can get away with anything. There's one in our neighborhood that does.

Morals don't mean a thing to him. He's unmarried and lives openly with a woman he's crazy about; and he doesn't care what the neighbors say or think. He has no regard for truth or law.

The duties of the so-called good citizen are just so much bunk as far as he's concerned. He doesn't vote at either the primaries or the general election. He never thinks of paying a bill.

We have seen him take a $2.00 taxi ride without giving the driver so much as a pleasant look. The driver only stared at him and muttered something silly.

He won't work a lick; he won't go to church; he can't play cards, or dance or fool around with musical instruments or the radio. So far as is known, he has no intellectual or cultural interests at all.

He neglects his appearance terribly. He's so indolent he'd let the house burn down before he'd turn in an alarm. The telephone can ring itself to pieces and he wouldn't bother to answer it. Even on such controversial subjects as the liquor question, nobody knows exactly where he stands, because one minute he's dry and the next minute he's wet.

But we'll say this for him, in spite of all his faults he comes from a very good family.

He's our new baby.

— *Author unknown*

—•◆•◆•—

All the world's a stage,
And all the men and women merely players;
They have their exits and their entrances;
And one man in his time plays many parts,
His act being seven ages. At first, the infant.
Mewling and puking in the nurse's arms,

Then the whining school boy, with his satchel,
And shining morning face, creeping like snail
Unwillingly to school. And then, the lover,
Sighing like a furnace, with a woeful ballad
Made to his mistress' eyebrow. Then, a soldier,
Full of strange oaths, and bearded like the bard,
Jealous in honor, sudden and quick in quarrel,
Seeking the bubble reputation
Even in the cannon's mouth. And then, the
    justice,
In fair round belly with good capon lin'd,
With eyes severe, and beard of formal cut,
Full of wise saws and modern instances;
And so he plays his part. The sixth age shifts
Into the lean and slipper'd pantaloon,
With spectacles on nose and pouch on side;
His youthful hose well sav'd, a world too wide
For his shrunk shank; and his big manly voice,
Turning again toward childish treble, pipes
And whistles in his sound. Last scene of all,
That ends his strange eventful history,
Is second childishness, and mere oblivion;
Sans teeth, sans eyes, sans taste, sans everything.
        — *William Shakespeare, (As You Like It)*

For Little Boys

God bless all little tousle-headed boys,
    All Bold Explorers under Grown-Up skies,
All knobby knuckled devotees of noise,
    All Robin Hoods and Arthurs in disguise.

God bless all little boys with sunburned knees,
    Sworn enemies of garden plots and roses,
Who flaunt cowlicks in the breeze
    And wear large freckles spread across their noses!
        — *Sara Henderson Hay*

Cry of a Lonely Heart

I WANT a boy,
A small boy,
A not-so-very-tall boy,
A boy of ten, eleven, or perhaps thirteen,
 A boy that I can talk with,
 And take a long walk with,
Then home again, to chatter over what we've seen.

A GAY little square boy,
 A sure-of-playing-fair boy,
A boy I can mother, and humor, and pet;
 A boy who will love me,
 And never weary of me. . .
D'you know a boy like this I can get?

A MOTHERLESS, tired boy,
 An ambition-fired boy,
A boy that I can pamper in every small whim,
 A hungry little sad boy,
 A dirty little bad boy,
I want a boy. . . who needs me as I need him.

         — *E. Pearl Dancey*

Recipe for a Boy

Take one large, grassy field; a group of children; a dog or two; a pinch of brook and a few pebbles. Mix the children and dogs well together, put them in the field, stirring constantly. Pour the brook over the pebbles, sprinkle the field with flowers. Spread over all a deep blue sky and bake in the hot sun. When brown remove and set away to cool in the bathtub.

         — *Author unknown*

Long, Long Thoughts, Charles Parks. Courtesy of Brookgreen Gardens. Photo by Bobby Phillips.

A boy's will is the wind's will and the thoughts of youth are long, long thoughts.

— *A Lapland Song*

Just a Boy

After a male baby outgrows long dresses and triangles and is covered with so much dirt that relatives don't dare to kiss him, he becomes a boy.

A boy is nature's answer to that false belief that there is no such thing as perpetual motion.

A boy is a growing animal of superlative promise, who can swim like a fish, run like a deer, climb like a squirrel, balk like a mule, bellow like a bull, eat like a pig, or act like a jackass, according to climatic conditions.

A boy, if not washed too often and kept in a cool, quiet place after each accident, will survive broken bones, hornets, measles, fights, and nine helpings of pie.

A boy is a piece of skin stretched over an appetite; a noise covered with smudges. A boy is the problem of our times, the hope of the world.

Every boy born is evidence that God is not yet discouraged with men.

— Author unknown

―――•◆◆•▬――

Prayer for a Son

A prayer composed by the late General Douglas MacArthur will live on as a spiritual legacy to his 26-year-old son, Arthur. The prayer, written when the soldier-statesman was heading outnumbered U.S. forces in the Philippines in early 1942, was said many times at morning devotions:

"Build me a son, O Lord, who will be strong enough to know when he is weak, and brave enough to face himself when he is afraid; one who will be proud and unbending in honest defeat, and humble and gentle in victory.

"Build me a son whose wishes will not take the place

of deeds; a son who will know Thee—and that to know himself is the foundation stone of knowledge.

"Lead him, I pray, not in the path of ease and comfort, but under the stress and spur of difficulties and challenge. Here let him learn compassion for those who fail.

"Build me a son whose heart will be clear, whose goal will be high, a son who will master himself before he seeks to master other men, one who will reach into the future and not forget the past.

"And after all these things are his, add, I pray, enough of a sense of humor so that he may always be serious, yet never take himself too seriously. Give him humility, so that he may always remember the simplicity of true greatness, the open mind of true wisdom, and the meekness of true strength.

"Then I, his father, will dare to whisper, I have not lived in vain."

— *General Douglas MacArthur*

The Younger Generation

The man was talking about his daughter and her generation—the younger generation—and the words leapt from the pages of the book:

". . . I wouldn't blame anyone for a pretty raw opinion of modern girls. I have it myself. . . To be brief, they have gotten under my skin, if you know what that means. Janey's generation is beyond my understanding. They have developed something new. They are eliminating right and wrong. They have no respect for their parents, and so far as I can see very little affection. They have a positive hatred for all restraint. They will not stand to be controlled. They have no faith in our old standards. As a rule they have no religion. They wear indecent clothes, or

I might say very few clothes at all. They dance all night, drown themselves in booze, pet and neck indiscriminately, and most of them go the limit."

Sound familiar?

It could have been written by almost any modern author about the present younger generation, but I fear the words "pet" and "neck" pretty well date it to the flapper era. The passage was written by Zane Grey in 1927 in a book called *Lost Pueblo*. It doesn't necessarily reflect Grey's own attitude toward that generation of youth, but rather it probably reflects a mass opinion, something like we have today.

— Bob Terrell

The Fiftieth Boy

About one boy in fifty will remain after the feast and of his own accord offer to help clear the things up or wash the dishes. Do you know this Fiftieth Boy?. . . There are forty-nine boys who are seeking jobs; the job seeks the Fiftieth Boy.

The Fiftieth Boy makes glad the heart of his parents . . . . The Fiftieth Boy smooths the wrinkles out of his teacher's forehead, and takes the worry out of her mind. . . . All the grouches and sour-faces brighten when they see the Fiftieth Boy coming, for he is brave and cheery. . . . The forty-nine "didn't think;" the Fiftieth Boy thinks. The Fiftieth Boy makes a confidant of his mother and a pal of his father.. . . He does not lie, steal or tattle, because he does not like to.. . . When he sees a banana peel on the sidewalk, where it is liable to cause someone to slip and fall, or a piece of glass in the road where it might puncture a tire, he picks it up.. . . The forty-nine think it's none of their business.. . . The Fiftieth Boy is a good sport.. . . He does not whine when he loses. He does not sulk when another wins the prize. He does not cry when

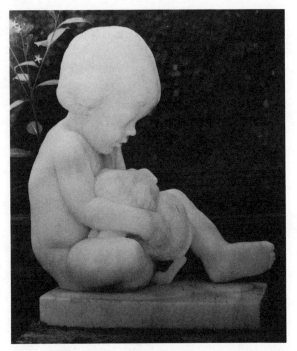

Susan, Edward Hoffman. Courtesy of Brookgreen Gardens.

In every child that's born, under no matter what
circumstance, and of no matter what parents, the
potentiality of the human race is born again.

— *James Agee*

he is hurt.. . . He is respectful to all women and girls.. . .
He is not afraid to do right or ashamed to be decent.. . .
He looks you straight in the eye.. . . He tells the truth,
whether the consequences to him are unpleasant or not.
. . . He is not a prig nor a sissy, but he stands up straight,
and is honest.. . . Forty-seven out of the forty-nine like
him.. . . He is pleasant toward his own sister as toward
the sisters of other fellows.. . . He is not sorry for himself.
. . . He works hard as he plays.. . . Everybody is glad to
see him.. . . Do you have that kind of boy at your house?
. . . If not, don't complain, there are not enough of them
to go around.

— *Dr. Frank Crane*

To INFINITE patience add a little wisdom carefully strained through profitable experience. Pour in a brimming measure of the milk of human kindness, and season well with salt of common sense. Boil gently over a friendly fire made of fine enthusiasm, stirring constantly with just discipline. When it has boiled long enough to be thoroughly blended, transfuse it by wise teaching to the eager mind of the restless boy and set away to cool. Tomorrow he will greet you an educated man.

— *Edwin Osgood Grover*

A Code for Teenagers

There is much to say in favor of a teenager's code written by teenager Virginia Chose of Dallas Texas. This code, which has appeared in the public press as far north as the Boston Globe, would be helpful to both teenagers and parents alike, for it puts into words what many think and feel.

1. Don't let your parents down. They brought you up.
2. Stop and think before you drink.
3. Ditch dirty thoughts fast or they'll ditch you.
4. Show-off driving is juvenile. Don't act your age.
5. Be smart, obey. You'll give orders yourself someday.
6. Choose your friends carefully. You are what they are.
7. Choose a date fit for a mate.
8. Don't go steady unless you're ready.
9. Go to church regularly. God gives you a week. Give Him back an hour.
10. Live carefully. The soul you save may be your own.

A woman is not old as long as she loves and is loved.

— *Vincent Van Gogh*

Poor Man

Man comes into this world without his consent, and leaves it against his will. During his stay on earth, most of his time is spent in one continual round of perplexities and misunderstandings.

In his infancy, he is an angel. In his boyhood he is a devil. In his manhood he is everything from a lizard up.

He may be a smart man, but in some folks' estimation he is a fool. If he raises a big family, he is a chump. If he raises a check he is a thief, and then the law raises cain with him. If he is a poor man, he is a bad manager and has no sense; if he is a rich man he is dishonest, but is considered smart.

If he goes to church he is a hypocrite; if he stays away from church, he is a sinner and damned. If he donates to foreign missions, he does it for a show; if he doesn't, he is stingy and a tightwad.

When he first comes into this world, everybody want to kiss him; before he goes out of it they all want to kick him.

If he dies young, there was a great future before him; if he lives to a ripe old age he is in the way, and is only living to save funeral expenses.

— Author unknown

Youth

The growing laxity of personal morals has always startled everyone over fifty. The increasing confusion in education, the chaotic changes which are coming over the governments of the world, have alarmed every thinking man in a dozen different generations.

If you read Spengler or Huizinga and take them seriously, you will want to give up now; you will want to

climb into the ark, shut the door, and ride the flood. But
that is because you belonged to a mature generation. You
have been battered by years; you are conscious of difficulties, wearied by problems, and depressed by the logic
which tells you that if things go on as they are, civilization
will fly apart.

Fortunately, however, there is always an element in
the world too young to worry. There is always a surge of
life coming from below, strong, confident, happy—and
ignorant. But part of youth's ignorance is a blessing in
disguise; for the difficulties and complexities which we
older ones have watched accumulating over the years
present, for them, normal problems. This they proceed
to attack with forces we no longer possess and, as a result,
somehow the world keeps turning.

And to help them, there is always in the background
"a divinity that shapes our ends." an all-wise, all-happy,
and all-powerful God, who has a very mysterious and
wonderful way of bringing good out of evil.

— *Rev. Robert J. Gannon, former president, Fordham*
University.

Youth

I must laugh and dance and sing,
Youth is such a lovely thing.

Soon I shall be old and stately;
I shall promenade sedately.

Down a narrow pavement street,
And the people that I meet

Will be stiff and narrow, too,
Careful of what they say and do;

It will be quite plain to see
They were never young like me.

The Spirit of American Youth, Donald DeLue.
Courtesy of Brookgreen Gardens.

     I must laugh and dance and sing,
     Youth is such a lovely thing.
               — Hughes Mearns

    When I walk where flowers grow
    I shall have to stoop down low

    If I want one for a prize;
    Now I'm just the proper size.

    Let me laugh and dance and sing,
    Youth is such a lovely thing.
               — Hughes Mearns

Girl by a Pool, Frances Grimes, South Carolina. Courtesy of Brookgreen Gardens.

A child more than any other gift
That earth can offer to declining man,
Brings hope with it and forward looking thoughts.
— *William Wordsworth*

Not long ago while visiting Mars Hill College, I had occasion to have lunch in the college dining room.

The room was crowded but I finally found a long table where three uneaten lunches had been set. Soon four girls came in, one bringing her plate. I was pleasantly surprised to see them close their eyes in silent prayer. I introduced myself and expressed my pleasure at seeing their act of devotion.

The girls were an inspiration, and the conversation was effortless. Being seventy-eight years old, I talked to them as a father to his children.

As I recall, here are some of the things I said in the twenty minutes we were there:

"I have a feeling that you look at my wrinkles and bald head and dread to think of the time when you might be the same age—a time not too far from the inevitable end of us all, with no joy or purpose or hope. Don't believe this, girls. I know more about the problems of your age than you do about mine, as I have experienced both. There are many stages of life; Shakespeare narrates seven. I am not sure one age is better than another, as each has its own joys and sorrows. Your age is in many ways the most trying of your life. You are so conscious of your peers' opinions, and wonder what you should do with your life.

"The pressures are so great, so hard to stand alone when you know you should, so many temptations to lead you wrong. I have been told that there are more suicides at your age than at any other. As we pass from one stage to another we tend to lose one set of joys and sorrows and take on another, with 'bright intervals' at every stage if we look for them. Learn to love, to work, to create, to see good things unfold under your hands and influence. While you cannot solve all the problems of the world, you can get a thrill from the challenge involved, and light a little candle in the darkness."

Shakespeare says, "See how far the little candle throws its beam; so shines a good deed in an evil world."

I told them how I had just lost my dear wife, to me the most wonderful woman in the world; how after being in a coma for several days, she opened her eyes, pulled my face down to hers, kissed my cheek, and closed her eyes again for the last time. She knew I loved her during the fifty years we spent together, but I wish I had told her so more often. Recently I have been telling my best friends, "I love you."

"Girls, when you go home next time, put your arms around your father and mother and tell them, 'I love you.' You will surprise them, but what a thrill it will be!"

Time came for classes and they had to go; one of them wept. Each of them shook my hand and said, "I love you, Mr. Phillips." One girl who sat on my side of the table put her arms around my neck and kissed me. It was only then that I noticed that I hadn't eaten my lunch, and it was cold.

— *R.B. Phillips*

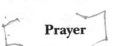

Prayer

LORD thou knowest better than I myself that I am growing older, and will someday be old.

KEEP ME from getting talkative, and particularly from the fatal habit of thinking I must say something on every subject on every occasion.

RELEASE ME from craving to try to straighten out everybody's affairs.

MAKE ME thoughtful, but not moody; helpful, but not bossy. With my vast store of wisdom it seems a pity not to use it all. . . but thou knowest, Lord, that I want a few friends at the end.

KEEP MY mind free from the recital of endless details . . . give me wings to get to the point.

SEAL MY lips to my aches and pains . . . they are increasing and my love of rehearsing them is becoming sweeter as the years go by.

I ASK for grace enough to listen to the tales of others' pains. Help me to endure them with patience.

TEACH ME the glorious lesson that occasionally it is possible that I may be mistaken. Keep me reasonably sweet, I do not want to be a saint. . . some of them are so hard to live with, but a sour old person is one of the crowning works of the devil.

HELP ME to extract all possible fun out of life. There are so many funny things around us and I don't want to miss any of them. AMEN.

— *Ray Kasten*

The Delights of Not Going

One of the delights known to age and beyond the grasp of youth is that of Not Going. When we are young it is almost agony not to go. We feel we are being left out of life, that the whole wonderful procession is sweeping by, probably forever, while we are weeping or sulking behind bars. Not to have an invitation—for the dance, the party, the match, the picnic, the excursion, the gang on holiday—is to be diminished, perhaps kept at midget's height for years. To have an invitation, and then not to be able to go—oh cursed spite! Thus we torment ourselves in the April of our time. Now in my early November not only do I not care the rottenest fig whether I receive an invitation or not, but after having carelessly accepted the invitation I can find delight in knowing that I am Not Going. I arrived at this by two stages. At the first, after years of illusion, I finally decided I was missing nothing by not going. Now, at the second, and, I hope, final stage, I stay away and no longer care whether I am missing anything or not. But don't I like to enjoy myself? On the contrary, by Not Going, that is just what I am trying to do.

— J.B. Priestly.

Rabbi Ben Ezra

Grow old along with me!
The best is yet to be,
The last of life, for which the
First was made:
Our times are in His hand
Who saith, "A whole I planned,
Youth shows but half; trust God:
See all nor be afraid."

— Robert Browning

Vacations of a Minute. . . .

Slow me down, Lord! Ease the pounding of my heart by the quieting of my mind. Steady my hurried pace with the vision of the eternal reach of time. Give me, amidst the confusion of my day, the calmness of the everlasting hills. Break the tensions of my nerves and muscles with the soothing music of the singing streams that live in my memory. Help me to know the magical, restoring power of sleep. Teach me the art of taking minute vacation.. . . of slowing down to look at a flower, to chat with a friend, to pat a dog, to read a few lines from a good book.

Remind me each day of the fable of the hare and the tortoise that I may know that the race is not always to the swift; that there is more to life than increasing its speed. Let me look upward into the branches of the towering oak and know that it grew great and strong because it grew slowly and well.

Slow me down, Lord, and inspire me to send my roots deep into the soil of life's enduring values that I may grow toward the stars of my greater destiny.

— *John G. Kilpack*

Life Begins at Seventy

Between the ages of 70 and 83 Commodore Vanderbilt added about $100 million to his fortune.

Oliver Wendell Holmes at 79 wrote *Over the Teacups.*

Cato at 80 began the study of Greek.

Goethe at 80 completed *Faust.*

Tennyson at 83 wrote *Crossing the Bar.*

Titian at 98 painted his historic picture of the Battle of Lepanto.

At 88, John Wesley preached every day.

Michelangelo painted the ceiling of the Sistine Chapel in his later 80s.

Benjamin Franklin went to France to serve his country at 78 and wrote his autobiography when over 80.

Thomas Jefferson was active in public life until his death at the age of 83.

Paderewski at 79 played the piano superbly before large audiences.

Stradivarius made his finest violins between 60 and 70 and continued making them up to his 93rd year.

Grandma Moses, who began painting at 79, is the most outstanding primitive artist of our time.

Henry Lytton, president of the Hub, a big Chicago store, retired at 83. At 87 he came back into the business and was still there at 100.

Look around you and find many others with notable achievements in later life.

— from (The Golden Book)

Justice between Generations

Every generation requires a strategy for its old age. An odd and chilling folktale that has been recited throughout Europe since the thirteenth century shows how far-reaching the repercussions of such strategies can be. "The Tale of the Ungrateful Son" begins with a description of an old merchant who day by day grows more infirm. The old man's wife has long since passed away, and he is miserably lonely. Fearing that he will soon lose his powers of mind, the old man finally decides to ask his middle-aged son and daughter-in-law if he might move in with their family, in the country.

At first the couple is overjoyed, for by way of compensation the merchant promises to bequeath his small fortune to them before he dies. But the old man in his dotage becomes increasingly troublesome to clean and feed. Eventually his daughter-in-law grows resentful of his constant needs and senile character. Indeed, she harangues her husband night and day, until he reluctantly agrees that the time has come to take the old man to the barn.

The ungrateful son is too embarrassed, however, to confront his father directly with his shameful decision. He gives that chore to his own youngest child.

"Take your grandfather to the barn and wrap him in the best horse blanket we have on the farm," he tells the boy. "That way the old man will be as comfortable as possible until he dies."

With tears in his eyes the child does as he is told, except that, having selected the farm's best horse blanket, he tears it in half. He uses one part to swaddle his beloved grandfather but sets the other part aside. The merchant's son is furious when he learns what the child has done. "What sort of boy are you who would put his own grandfather out in the barn to freeze with only half a horse blanket?" he shouts.

"But father," the child replies, "I am saving the other half for you."

— *Phillip Longman*

———•◆◆◆•———

Some Ageist Myths Never Die

Misconceptions about aging persevere. Below are some myths mentioned at this year's American Academy of Neurology's Annual Meeting, followed by some interesting rebuttals.

• Old age takes all the fun out of life. "When (people) complain like that, the fault is one of character, not years. Old (people) who exercise self-discipline, who are not peevish or insensitive, find old age quite bearable."

- Old age causes your memory to fail. "No doubt it does, if you don't keep it in trim or if you're born a trifle dull. I'm not worried by the saying, 'Read tombstones and lose your memory.' It's by reading those stones that I refresh my memory of the dead."
- Old age deprives us of all pleasures. "The (person) who sits in the first row of the theater enjoys it more, but the one who sits in the last row still enjoys it."
- Old age diminishes strength. "I never liked that proverb, 'Get an old head early if you want an old head long.' There are some invalids who can't participate in life's activities, but such disability isn't peculiar to old age; it is rather the usual concomitant of ill health."
- Old age means death is near. "What could be more in accord with the Law of Nature than for the old to die? Fruits, if they are green, must be forcefully pulled from the bough, but if they are ripe and mellow, they drop off."

The myths were cited by the meeting's experts as old stereotypes that persist today. The rebuttals are those of the Roman philosopher Cicero in 45–44 B.C.

— American Academy of Neurology

━•◆◆•▬

Jenny Kissed Me

Jenny kissed me when we met,
Jumping from the chair she sat in;
Time, you thief, who love to get
Sweets into your list, put that in!
Say I'm weary, say I'm sad,
Say that health and wealth have missed me,
Say I'm growing old, but add,
Jenny kissed me.

— Leigh Hunt

When You Are Old

When you are old, and life has filled behind you,
Pictures of youth appear and still remind you
Of bygone days, of carefree days,
When your heart was king,
A wonderful thing, but just a little crazy.

Nothing on earth can rob you of your mem'ries,
Never the same are things as one is aging,
So live and love, your youth is gold,
Then you may live in your heart when you are old.
                                    — *C. Robert Jones, (Rivals)*

Even if I knew that tomorrow the world would go to pieces, I would still plant my apple tree.
                                    — *Martin Luther*

Some Meaningful Principles
I Have Learned
in the Last 85 Years

1. No one can hold malice toward another who refused to hold malice toward him. Love when applied is stronger than hatred.
2. People respect us for our great accomplishments; they love us for our little kindnesses.
3. Happiness does not come by seeking it; it is the result of benevolent actions.
4. We need a good "forgetter" as much as a good memory. We need to learn to "keep that which is worth keeping, and with a breath of kindness, throw the rest away."
5. Our standard of conduct and life-style should not be determined by society around us.

6. We become what we are by the ability and talents with which we are born plus what we are exposed to through our five basic senses.
7. Perfection is a virtue we may work toward but never fully attain.
8. Education is power and is therefore dangerous if not guided by strong moral and spiritual virtues.
9. We need some time to ourselves; it is so easy to lose our way in this complex world.
10. Long life does not assure a good life.

The Talmud says there are three things one should do in the course of one's life: have a child, plant a tree, and write a book. With the help of a gracious Heavenly Father and the charity and encouragement of my friends, I have attained these goals—however imperfectly. It may well be that whatever success one attains is due not so much because *of the vicissitudes of life but* in spite of *them.*

— *R.B. Phillips*

Riders of the Dawn, A.A. Weinman. Courtesy of Brookgreen Gardens. Photo: Bobby Phillips.

And God said, Let there be light: and there was light.
— *Genesis 1:3*

EDUCATION

*Nobody wishes to be opposed to the flag, moth-
erhood, apple pie or education. After twenty-five years
of experience in public school administration, I am sure
education ought to be promoted and encouraged, but
the objectives ought to be redefined. It seems to me that
both the home and school have been led to believe that
there is some magic way for a child to get an education
in totally pleasant surroundings, that there is some
"royal road to learning." We have drifted into the fallacy
of thinking that we just need training for a well-paying
job, so that we can purchase abundant living. We need
to stress the humanities so we can take advantage of
what others have learned about life.*

———•◆•◆•———

Man, if he enjoys a right education and happy environment, becomes the most alive and civilized of all
beings. But he is the most savage of all products, if he is
inadequately and improperly trained.

— *Plato*

———•◆◆•———

Life is no brief candle to me. It is a sort of splendid
torch which I have got hold of for the moment, and I
want to make it burn as brightly as possible before hand-
ing it on to the future generations.

— *George Bernard Shaw*

25

Who Are the Educated People?

A proud young mother asked General Lee what advice he would offer in the rearing of her son. In that thoughtful way of his, Lee paused and answered, "Teach him to deny himself." Lee was a learned man and his education, as well as his long career in armies, had taught him that denial is at the heart of education.

The answer depends on motivation. To what purpose do we plan to put our learning? In the long view, education, like virtue, is its own reward. But if we must view it in a pragmatic sense, it can be said that its most worthy purpose is to make us more humane creatures in an age when technology and our own avarice move us away from the advice of General Lee.

Many of us equate higher education with Saturday's hero—"Win one for the Gipper." Or if our community somehow can find the money to build a new football stadium, we smugly believe our town has done its bit for the education of the young. (Philosopher Elbert Hubbard wrote, "Football bears the same relation to education that bullfighting does to agriculture.")

Few of us, and I'm guilty, too, stop to think through what an education really is. What we have in America, at best, is a trained population, not really an educated one. A harsh judgment, perhaps, but true.

It is not enough to learn. Learning has to be passed on to the young. If we have one duty above all others it is the obligation to teach the young logic and sympathy. As George Will reminds us, "A world without sympathy would be a cold place indeed."

The Founding Fathers believed that the future of the republic rested in the hands of an educated people. They viewed education and democracy as inseparable. And part of their perception was rooted in the truism that restraint, moderation, and self-denial—the virtues ironically exemplified in another age by Robert E. Lee—would help enable the United States to fulfill the noblest experiment in self-government in the annals of the human family. We have a long way to go, don't you think?

— *Rick Gunter*

The chief purpose of education is to train the mind and will to do the work you need to do when it ought to be done whether you like to do it or not.

— *Thomas Huxley*

The Sower, Joseph Charles Fleri. Courtesy of Brookgreen Gardens. Photo: Bobby Phillips.

If we work on marble, it will perish . . . but if we work on immortal minds . . . we engrave on those tablets something that will brighten to all eternity.

— *Daniel Webster*

Response

We are all blind until we see
That in the human plan
Nothing is worth the making
If it does not make the man.
Why build these cities glorious,
If man unbuilded goes?
In vain we build the world, unless
The builder also grows.

— *Author unknown*

Education does not make us smarter; it merely propels us further and faster in the direction of our naive abilities, and if one's ability is to make a fool of himself, education can help him do a magnificent job of that.

— *Sidney Harris*

A Teacher Speaks

I must not interfere with any child, I have been told,
To bend his will to mine, or try to shape him through
    some mold
Of thought. Naturally as a flower he must unfold.
Yet flowers have the discipline of wind and rain,
And tho I know it gives the gardener much pain,
I've seen him use his pruning shears to gain
More strength and beauty for some blossoms bright.
And he would do whatever he thought right
To save his flowers from a deadening blight.
I do not know—yet it does seem to me
That only weeds unfold just naturally.

— *Alice Gay Judd*

Education does not mean teaching people what they do not know. It means teaching them to behave as they do not behave.

— *John Ruskin*

———•◆•———

The following rules and regulations for the government of the Board of Superintendents of Common Schools in the County of Chathan, North Carolina appeared in "Common Schools, Proceedings of the Board of Superintendents," 1841–1864:

1. It shall be the duty of the Chairman to organize the Board at 12 o'clock under a penalty of $1.00.
2. It shall be the duty of the Chairman to see that good order be kept in the room where the Board meets under a penalty of $2.00 and the Board shall consider themselves bound to sustain him.
3. If two or more members rise to address the chair at the same time he shall decide who has a right to the floor.
4. The Chairman shall not suffer any person to speak upon any subject but the members of the Board unless by permission of the Board.
5. If the Chairman shall violate any of the rules of the Board it shall be his duty to leave the chair and the Board shall call one of its members to the chair to preside until his case is disposed of.
6. It shall be the duty of the C.S.C. to attend in the room at 12 o'clock under a penalty of $2.00.
7. If any of the Board shall fail to meet in the room at the time appointed he shall be fined $2.00.
8. If any member shall absent himself from the room after the house is called to order without the consent of the chair he shall pay the sum of $1.00. The Board shall hear all excuses and if they are of opinion that they are good the member shall be excused.

9. No member shall address the chair sitting under a penalty of 25¢ for every such offense.
10. No member shall speak twice on the same subject until all of them have had an opportunity to do the same.
11. If any member shall use disrespectful language or conduct he shall be fined at the discretion of the Board.

Governor Berkley wrote to England in 1670 as follows:

I thank God there are no free schools nor printing; and I hope we shall not have them these hundred years; for learning has brought disobedience and heresy and sects into the world; and printing has divulged them and libels against the government. God keep us from both.

Baby specialist Dr. Benjamin Spock blames teachers, psychologists, social workers, and physicians—himself included—for helping parents lose their self-assurance in dealing with their children.

Spock says parents aren't firm enough with their children for fear of losing their love or incurring their resentment.

Parents have been persuaded that only trained persons know how children should be reared, he said in the current Redbook magazine.

"This is a cruel deprivation that we professionals have imposed on mothers and fathers," Spock said. "Of course, we did it with the best of intentions. . . we didn't realize, until it was too late, how our know-it-all attitude was undermining the self-assurance of parents."

Parents are prone, for example, to letting slip without

comment a child's failure to obey a simple wish, such as refraining from a second piece of candy, he said.

"They're afraid that if they insist, their children will resent them or at least won't love them as much," he said.

"The way to get a child to do what must be done or stop doing what shouldn't be done is to be clear and definite each time."

— *Associated Press news release*

Jack be nimble, Jack be quick
Snap the blade and give it a flick;
Grab the purse, it's easy done.
Then for kicks, just for fun,
Plunge the knife, and cut and run.

The above quotation was published by "The Asheville Citizen" in 1986. Quoted from Inner City Mother Goose, *Simon & Schuster, 1969, page 26* Language 8, *an eighth grade composition textbook.*

In Laidlaw Language Program, *Teacher's Edition, 1983, page 147, it is suggested that this poem be a model for the style of writing for eighth grade students.*

How low can our educational leadership stoop to recommend this textbook?

Without education they will lack the taste to desire a better standard of living. Without education they will lack the talent to obtain a better standard of living. And without education they will lack the character to keep a better standard even if they obtain it. Whatever the immediate answers for the South, the long one, the great one is still education. There are few, if any, people who need to be ignorant. The question is—do people want it? If they do, they can get it.

— *John Temple Graves II*

The following objects of primary education, pre-
pared by Thomas Jefferson, were recorded in a report
of the Carnegie Foundation for the Advancement of
Teaching:

To give every citizen the information he needs for the transaction of his own business;

To enable him to calculate for himself, and to express and preserve his ideas, his contracts and accounts, in writing;

To improve, by reading, his morals and faculties;

To understand his duties, to his neighbors and country, and to discharge with competence the functions confided to him by either;

To know his rights; to exercise with order and justice those he retains; to choose with discretion the fiduciary of those he delegates; and to notice their conduct with diligence, with candor, and judgment;

And, in general, to observe with intelligence and faithfulness all the social relations under which he shall be placed.

Grow Up and Go Home

Always we hear the plaintive cry of the teenager: "What can we do? Where can we go?" The answer is, GO HOME.

Hang the storm windows, paint the woodwork, rake the leaves, mow the lawn, shovel the walk, wash the car, learn to cook, scrub some floors, repair the sink, build a boat, get a job.

Help the minister, the Red Cross, the Salvation Army, visit the sick, assist the poor, study your lessons, and when you are through and not too tired, read a book.

Your parents do not owe you entertainment. Your city or village does not owe you a living. You owe the world something. You owe it your time and energy and your talents so no one will be at war, in poverty or lonely again.

In plain simple words—GROW UP! Quit being a cry-baby. Get out of your dream world and develop a backbone, not a wishbone, and start acting like a man or a lady.

You're supposed to be mature enough to accept some of the responsibilities your parents have carried for years. They have nursed, protected, helped, begged, excused, tolerated, and denied themselves needed comforts so that you could have every benefit.

IN HEAVEN'S NAME—GROW UP AND GO HOME.

— *Judge Gilliam, (WBTV editorial, December 28, 1965)*

Booker T. Washington. Courtesy of Tuskegee University. Photo: Walter Scott.
Booker T. Washington lifting the veil of ignorance from his own people.

Dr. Detlev W. Bronk, one of the nation's leading scientists, makes this appraisal:

"People are rich with power and goods beyond the dreams of kings. . . They have to be inspired."

"Give every student the greatest challenge he can meet."

"Set standards above what people think they want."

"The great majority of people don't want things too easy."

----•◆◆•▬

Ten Tips For Parents

The police department in Houston, Texas, has obviously become a little fed up with all those freewheeling kids in all those Cadillacs. So somebody on the force has prepared a message to parents. It's entitled, "How To Raise a Delinquent," and it goes like this:

1. Begin at infancy to give the child everything he wants. In this way he will grow up to believe the world owes him a living.
2. When he picks up bad words, laugh at him. This will make him think he's cute.
3. Never give him any spiritual training. Wait until he is 21 and then let him "decide for himself."
4. Pick up everything he leaves lying around—books, shoes, clothes. Do everything for him so that he will be experienced in throwing all responsibility to others.
5. Quarrel frequently in his presence. In this way he will not be too shocked when the home is broken later.
6. Give a child all the spending money he wants. Never let him earn his own. Why should he have things as tough as you had them?
7. Satisfy his every craving for food, drink, and comfort. Denial may lead to harmful frustrations.

8. Take his part against neighbors, teachers, policemen. They are all prejudiced against your child.
9. When he gets into trouble, apologize for yourself by saying, "I never could do anything with him."
10. Prepare for a life of grief. You are bound to have it.

—■·●◆●·■—

Sports As Our Opium

If Karl Marx, who died 100 years ago, were still alive today, he might be sorely tempted to revise his famous slur, "Religion is the opium of the people."

It is no longer true, if it ever was, for something else has taken its place, at least in our country. Today, sport has become the opium of the people.

The playing of games is no longer a diversion, a hobby, a pleasant respite from weightier matters. It has turned into a religion, a business, a central concern for the great mass of American men, high, low, and in between.

While it may be true that religion, in the past, narcoticized many, it also awakened many others to their social and moral responsibilities. Sport has no such redeeming aspect in our society.

It has little to do with games as such any more, which were devised to refresh the human spirit. It has turned into a passion, a mania, a drug far more potent and widespread than any mere chemical substance. It inflates its participants, inflames its spectators, and enriches its promoters beyond the dreams of avarice.

It has transformed a pastime into an industry, a personal contest into a commercial spectacle, a physical prowess into a form of worship. It encourages not good sportsmanship, but greed, cunning, brutality, chicanery, disputation, gambling, and rotten manners on the parts of the players as well as the audiences.

Sports is as necessary, as useful, as nourishing to humans as any other natural activity—but it is no longer a natural activity; in its cancerous form, it has displaced religion, dislodged citizenship and even further dislocated communication between the sexes.

We have lost our sense of proportion about what is important in life because our realistic situation seems so formidable, so taxing and vexing, so almost insoluble, that it is simpler to focus our energies and allegiances on the playing fields. And we shall pay a heavy price for this in the end.

— Sidney J. Harris

A Good Teacher

In addition to the three R's many other values quite as important should be taught or "caught."

There is no adequate way to test the value of a good teacher by means of tests or criteria. The intangible traits of character such as love, kindness, joy, beauty, goodness, unselfishness, the joy of a job well done, tenacity, inspiration, and many others are even more important than a set of facts presented. Certain facts are part of the necessary tools to be used in the process of obtaining a good education; but facts alone, without character, are a hazard to a decent society. With all due respect to scientific advancement in the last generation, it is power and can be used for good or evil. For the first time in the history of the world, man has power enough to destroy the world. So far as we know from the study of history, man has always used whatever power he had to destroy the "enemy." If we do not develop enough moral character to direct this vast power, I shudder to think of the consequence.

Perhaps we should redefine the meaning of education in the classroom. On July 12, 1985, the following news item appeared in the Asheville Citizen. I quote in part:

Wilson Goode, son of a Northampton, North Carolina, sharecropper and first black mayor of Philadelphia, told educators at a State Department of Public Instruction meeting at Grove Park Inn in Asheville, North Carolina, how his early schooling shaped his life. Textbook facts are not mentioned.

"My teachers cared about me," he began. "They were interested in my learning—and my achievement. They taught me the value of education, and it became clear to me that the key to my future was to have an overall thirst for knowledge."

"They taught me respect for authority, my teachers, all elders, and yes, my government," he continued. "They taught me to respect myself more than anything else. I never understood why each day my teachers would inspect me. They looked at my ears, my hair, to see if my face was washed. Basically, it said to me the way I looked was important."

"As I look at the road I've traveled since that time—I go back to these five things:
1. Discipline
2. Respect for authority
3. Respect for my parents, teachers, and elders
4. Respect for government
5. Respect for myself."

Goode's father was a sharecropper who never learned to read and write. his mother quit school to work on the farm. His grandparents and great-grandparents were born into slavery.

Working With Mind

If we work upon marble, it will perish; if we work upon brass, time will efface it; if we rear temples, they will crumble into dust; but if we work upon immortal minds, if we imbue them with principles, with the just fear of God and love of our fellow men, we engrave on those tablets something that will brighten to all eternity.

— *Daniel Webster*

Give me the education of the children for a generation and I will make war impossible.

— *Benjamin Kidd*

Were half the power that fills the world with terror,
Were half the wealth bestowed on camps and courts,
Given to redeem the human mind from error,
There were no need for arsenals and forts. . .

— *Henry Wadsworth Longfellow*

Who Will Use Force?

For every person who says, "I don't come to church because I was forced as a child," I can name you a hundred who say, "I come to church now because I was made to as a child."

It's not, "Johnny, would you like to go to choir rather than watch TV?" but rather, "Johnny, we've enrolled you in the choir. Get your coat—let's go."

Someone is going to force your child. If it's not you— then it will have to be teacher, policeman, or warden. Someone has said their are four pieces of wood necessary to raise a boy—a baseball bat, a plow handle, a church pew, and a paddle. All are essential.

— *Dr. John Ladia, First Baptist Church,*
Clarksville, Tennessee

Dear Son:

For your Christmas, I hereby give to you—for your very own, to use as you will—one hour of my time every day.

Your Father
— *Author unknown*

What a real present! What a wise father! What a lucky boy! So many dads buy their boys off with a transient toy, or a crinkly bank note. How few give to their sons themselves.

———•·•◆•·•▬—

. . . Rather than continuing to make the scapegoat the beleaguered teacher, let the finger point to the one who looks into the mirror, and that includes each youth.

The present trend in American life, with games, sports, and, above all, television, has distracted parents from their parental responsibility: to pass on our heritage, our culture, to their children.

Few parents read anymore with their children or assist them in selecting good books to enrich their inquisitive minds. A house without books is like a room without windows.

Television is a "plug-in-drug" and parents should "take a hammer in the right hand and swing it at the damned thing."

I would knock off sports in all public schools, these professional sports. After you've seen one football game, what more is there to see?

Teachers should be paid much higher salaries, and schools should stress language and mathematics. . .

— *Retired Adm. Hyman G. Rickover*

———•◆•·•▬—

Sonata. Courtesy of Brookgreen Gardens. Photo:
Bobby Phillips.

   The man who has no music in himself—
   Let no such man be trusted.
   — *William Shakespeare, (The Merchant of*
     Venice)

MUSIC

I never knew but one man who said he did not like music; he was a miserable old cuss who didn't like people either.

There is not a dearth of people who like music, but the type of music a person likes identifies his or her character. One man is reputed to have said, "Let me write the songs of this country and I'll determine its destiny."

The man that hath no music in himself,
Nor is not moved by the concord of sweet sound,
Is fit for treasons, strategies, and spoils;
The motions of his spirit are dull as night,
—And his affection dark as Erebus.
Let no such man be trusted.
— *William Shakespeare, (The Merchant of Venice)*

⬤

The value of good music is eternal—fixed as the stars. Nor does time diminish its value. The oldest known Christian hymn is sixteen and a half centuries old.

"I would rather have written that hymn (Jesus Lover of My Soul)," said Henry Ward Beecher, "than to have all the fame of all the kings that ever sat upon the earth."
— *Author unknown*

41

Night, Mario Korbel. Courtesy of Brookgreen Gardens. Photo: Bobby Phillips.

And the night shall be filled with music,
And the cares that infest the day,
Shall fold their tents like the Arabs,
And as silently steal away.
— *Henry Wadsworth Longfellow*

I Hear America Singing

I hear America singing, the varied carols I hear;
Those of mechanics—each one singing his, as it should
   be, blithe and strong;
The carpenter singing his, as he measures his plank or
   beam;
The mason singing his, as he makes ready for work, or
   leaves off work;
The boatman singing what belongs to him in his boat—
   the deckhand singing on the steamboat deck;
The shoemaker singing as he sits on his bench—the
   hatter singing as he stands;
The woodcutter's song—the plowboy's, on his way in the
   morning, or at the noon intermission, or at
   sundown;
The delicious singing of the mother—or of the young
   wife at work—or of the girl sewing or washing—
   each singing what belongs to her, and to none else;
The day what belongs to the day—at night, the party of
   young fellows, robust, friendly,
Singing, with open mouths, their strong melodious
   songs.

— Walt Whitman

The moon shines bright in such a night as this. . . .
How sweet the moonlight sleep upon this bank!
Here will we sit and let the sound of music
Creep into our ears; soft stillness and the night
Become the touches of sweet harmony.
Sit, Jessica, Look how the floor of heaven
Is thick with patines of bright gold;
There's not the smallest orb which those behold'st
But in his motion like an angel sings,
Still quiring to the young ey'd cherubims;
Such harmony is in immortal souls,
But whilst this muddy vesture of decay
Doth grossly close it in,
We cannot hear it.
— *William Shakespeare, (The Merchant of Venice)*

Because the road was steep and long,
And through a dark and lonely land,
God put upon my lips a song,
And put a lantern in my hand.
— *Joyce Kilmer*

Pipes of Pan, Louis St. Gaudens. Courtesy of Brookgreen Gardens.

If music be the food of love play on;
Give me excess of it.
— *William Shakespeare, (King Lear)*

Moonbeams, Abram Belskie. Courtesy of Brookgreen Gardens.

All things bright and beautiful,
All creatures great and small,
All things wise and wonderful,
The Lord God made them all.
— *Cecil Francis Alexander*

NATURE

When we think of nature we acknowledge two things—beauty and utility. Man has always been awed by the beauty and mystery of nature. Early man revered parts of it; all the ancient religions, especially those of the East, thought of nature as equal to themselves and failed to use the physical world for their own advancement.

Only with the coming of Christianity did man realize that he alone was the crown of all creation. In Genesis 1:28 the Bible says "and God blessed them and God said unto them, Be fruitful and multiply, and replenish the earth, and subdue it; and have dominion over the fish of the sea, and over the fowl of the air, and over every living thing that moveth upon the earth."

With the advent of the Christian religion man was first liberated from his slavery to nature and made aware of the fact that he himself was the crown of all God's creation and nature was to become his servant. Here was the genesis of not only man's liberation but his command to subdue the forces of nature; and thus the beginning of scientific investigation and development.

However, this command to subdue and use the forces of nature need not depreciate the beauty and wonder of God's creation.

Trees

A tree is patient; it never gets in a hurry.
A tree is strong; what's firmer than an oak?
A tree is useful; it's man's right hand in building.
A tree is busy; as long as it lives it grows.
A tree is obedient; it bends to the wind and responds to
    the sunshine.
A tree brings comfort; feel its shade on a hot day.
A tree is kind; it never envies another tree.
A tree endures; each acorn may produce another oak.
A tree is generous; it gives to the service of man.
A tree is thankful; it lifts its branches toward heaven.
A tree is beautiful; see its arch against the sky.
A tree is joyful; hear it sing with the wind.
A tree is free; who dares try to imprison it?
A tree is quiet; it resists the clatter of the street.
A tree is sincere; an oak never tries to be a poplar.
A tree is humble; it never prates its virtues.
A tree is musical; it ennobles the sound of the violin.
A tree is sacrificing; it gives itself to be burned.

— *R.B. Phillips*

---

from **Thanatopsis**

To him who in the love of nature holds
Communion with her visible forms, she speaks
A various language; for his gay hours
She has a voice of gladness, and a smile
And eloquence of beauty, and she glides
Into his darker musings, with a mild
And healing sympathy, that steals away
Their sharpness, ere he is aware.

— *William Cullen Bryant*

Boy and Frog, Elsie Ward Herring. Courtesy of Brookgreen
Gardens.

> Poems are made by fools like me,
> But only God can make a tree.
> — *Joyce Kilmer*

Trees

I think that I shall never see
A poem lovely as a tree.
A tree whose hungry mouth is pressed
Against the earth's sweet flowing breast!
A tree that looks at God all day,
And lifts her leafy arms to pray;
A tree that may in summer wear
A nest of robins in her hair;
Upon whose bosom snow has lain!
Who intimately lives with rain.
Poems are made by fools like me,
But only God can make a tree.
> — *Joyce Kilmer*

Beauty

A lily in the mossy glen,
So fresh and pure and white;
We tear apart to look within,
And spoil a pretty sight.
— *R.B. Phillips*

Let it not be said to your shame "This place was
beautiful until I came."
— *from a sign in Bellingraph Gardens, Mobile, Alabama*

Flower in the crannied wall,
I pluck you out of the crannies;
I hold you here, root and all, in my hand,
Little flower—but if I could understand
What you are, root and all, and all in all,
I should know what God and man is.
— *Alfred Lord Tennyson*

The World Is Too Much With Us

The world is too much with us: late and soon,
Getting and spending, we lay waste our powers:
Little we see in Nature that is ours;
We have given our hearts away, a sordid boom!
The sea that bares her bosom to the moon;
The winds that will be howling at all hours,
And are up-gathered now like sleeping flowers;
For this, for everything, we are out of tune;
It moves us not!
— *William Wordsworth*

Beautiful Pacific, Columbia Publishing.
    Break, break, break,
    On the cold gray stones,
    O sea!. . .
    But O for the touch of a vanished hand,
    And the sound of a voice that is still!
                 — *Alfred Lord Tennyson*

Apostrophe To The Ocean

There is a pleasure in the pathless woods,
There is a rapture in the lonely shore,
There is a society where none intrudes,
By the deep Sea, and Music in the roar;
I love not man less, but Nature more,
From these our interviewers which I steal.
From these I may be or have been before,
To mingle with the Universe and feel
What I can ne'er express, yet
Can not all conceal.
                 — *Lord Byron*

Constancy

At midnight now I lie awake
And hear the surging deep.
It claps its hands,
It laps its sands,
But never a pause to sleep.
I like to see you are so free
To keep God's laws in constancy.

When God made man
He gave a choice, a voice
His love to make or break.
Sometimes we fain would have our laws,
Fixed, immutable as the sea,
So evil would no longer trouble us,
Nor let us drift from Thee.

If this were so, we'd cease to grow,
Nor feel the need of Thee.
Lord God of hosts,
Forgive our fretful, frightful ways!
— *R.B. Phillips*

The Sea, Photographer unknown.
It claps its hands,
It laps its sands,
But never a pause to sleep
— *R.B. Phillips*

Whippoorwill

Every evening, just at sunset
When all the world is still,
Down from the marshes and valleys
Comes the cry of the whippoorwill.
"Whippoorwill! Whippoorwill!"

Just when twilight shadows thicken,
I hear him calling still—
Over the hills and mountains
His merry notes of "Whippoorwill!
Whippoorwill! Whippoorwill!"

His notes not heard in the daytime,
But when all the birds are still,
Out from the stillness of twilight
Comes the cry of "Whippoorwill!
Whippoorwill! Whippoorwill!"

Oh, why sing only at twilight, beautiful whippoorwill,
Piping your notes in the evening,
When all other birds are still?
Whippoorwill! Whippoorwill!

Oh, I have learned to love you,
And I shall love you till
The days grow cold in autumn,
And you hush your cry of "Whippoorwill."
Whippoorwill! Whippoorwill!

— R.B. Phillips

———•◆◆•—

Postscripts

A child hasn't really lived until he walks in the forest
in springtime, listens to the wind in the trees, and feels
the moss-covered earth beneath his feet. There is a feeling of being so near to God that you can almost hear the
whisper of His voice.

— Bob Terrell

Spring

My beloved spake, and said to me,
Rise up, my love, my fair one, and come away.
For lo, the winter is past,
The rain is over and gone;
The flowers appear on the earth;
The time of the singing of birds is come, and
The voice of the turtle is heard in our land;
The fig tree putteth forth her green figs,
And the vines with the tender grapes give a good smell.
— *Song of Solomon 2:10*

Nature

When springtime gives her gentle call
To every flower and tree;
They never hesitate at all,
But it's not so with me;
My life is not so free.
I grope and dig on ancient lore;
Its books and teachers I must see;
Yet nature teaches me much more
Than all the sages gone before.
— *R.B. Phillips*

Spring Is Here

Spring is here again!
I met her today in the pussy willow,
Swaying gracefully in the breeze;
I saw her in the gentle rain
As she washed the faces of my daffodils,
And tapped her rhythm on my window pane.

I heard her as I passed a marsh
Where little creatures chirped their joyful songs
And in the music of the brook by whose side
A meadowlark rehearsed a melody.

Ah Spring! You're such a welcome season.
I want to capture every sight and sound,
Hold you tightly in my memory until all my
Senses throb with the miracle of you!

— *Ruth Phillips*

Victory of Spring, Willarld Paddock. Courtesy of Brookgreen Gardens.

Spring is here again! I met her today in the pussy willow—

— *Ruth W. Phillips*

Ode

O ye fountains, meadows, hills, and groves,
Forbade not any severing of our loves!
Yet in my heart of hearts I feel your might;
I only have relinquished one delight,
To live beneath your more habitual sway,
I love the brooks which down their channels fret
Even more than when I tipped lightly as they;
The innocent brightness of a newborn day is lonely yet;
The clouds that gather round the setting sun
Do take a sober coloring from an eye
That hath kept watch o'er man's mortality;
Another race has been, and other palms are worn
Thanks to the human heart by which we live,
Thanks to its tenderness, its joys, and fears,
To me the meanest flower that blows can give
Thoughts that do often lie too deep for tears.

— William Wordsworth

Stranger In The Night

We were never told more eloquently than when Chief Sealth of the Duwanish Tribe in Washington told President Franklin Pierce in a letter in 1855.

Listen to his prophetic words of warning as reprinted in the Conservation News, voice of the National Wildlife Federation:

"The Great Chief in Washington sends word that he wishes to buy our land. How can you buy or sell the sky—the warmth of the land? The idea is strange to us. Yet we do not own the freshness of the air or the sparkle of the water.

"How can you buy them from us? Every part of this earth is sacred to my people. Every shiny pine needle, every sandy shore, every mist in the dark woods, every clearing and humming insect is holy in the memory and experience of my people.

"We know that white man does not understand our ways. One portion of the land is the same to him as the next, for he is a stranger who comes in the night and takes from the land whatever he needs. The earth is not his brother but his enemy, and when he has conquered it he moves on. He leaves his fathers' graves, and his children's birthright is forgotten.

"There is no quiet place in the white man's cities. No place to hear the leaves of spring or the rustle of insect wings. But perhaps because I am savage and do not understand—the clatter only seems to insult the ears.

"And what is there to life if a man cannot hear the lovely cry of the whippoorwill or the arguments of the frog around the pond at night.

"The whites, too, shall pass—perhaps sooner than other tribes. Continue to contaminate your bed and you will one night suffocate in your own waste. When the buffalo are all slaughtered, the wild horses tamed, the secret corners of the forest heavy with the scent of many men, and the view of the ripe hills blotted by talking wires.

"Where is the thicket? Gone. Where is the eagle? Gone. And what is to say good-bye to the swift and the hunt, the end of living and beginning of survival."

— *Bob Terrell*

———•◆◆•——

My Heart Leaps Up When I Behold

My heart leaps up when I behold a rainbow in the sky. So was it when my life began; So is it now I am a man; So be it when I shall grow old, Or let me die!

— *William Wordsworth*

Reminiscence

Honey, I won't be gone long—
Going up to the Flat Meadow
To please the roots of our sick flowers.
Up, up into the cozy cove of the Billy Mountain;
Soil, fresh, clean, black, deep, gentle—kind to all life;
A billion years in forming,
Mother Nature taking patient pride in its creation,
Intending nothing else than feeding hungry plants.

Wait a minute, Honey; I may be gone longer;
I may just want to stay a special spell.
Memories of my childhood shout to me.
Just now this soil is mine—
Will be as long as my Father gives me life.
Nature's bounty was not spread out for only one.
It's here for none to waste, but all to use.

Three generations have I known and tilled this soil.
I've seen the hills and heard the sounds;
Smelled the fragrance and tasted joy and sorrow.
I've known life and death of loved ones;
Tried to live to deserve the best of eternity sure to come.
Here on the Billy Mountain is the place to:
        Paint a picture,
        write a poem,
        sing a song,
        hear a symphony,
        have a romance,
        —such ecstasy!
        —such memories!
Forgive me, Honey, for being late!

Just above the Flat Meadow is the mountain peak—
Pointing upward like a slender arrow,
Shimmering in the sunlight.
From this peak, with a measure of imagination,
I see most of the "spots" in Mitchell County—

To name a few:
>   Harrell Hill, Mine Creek, Duck Branch, Loafers'
>   Glory, Toecane, Bakersville, Cane Creek, Rock
>   Creek, Hawk, Clarissa, McKinney Cove, Young's
>   Cove, Iron Mountain, Greasy Creek, Spring Creek,
>   Frog Level, View Mountain, Roan Mountain, Glen
>   Ayre, Hack Mountain, Double Island, Burnsville,
>   Mt. Mitchell, George's Fork, Boonford, Snow Hill,
>   Wing, Lily Branch, Squally, Swiss, Hardscrabble,
>   Ball Creek, Deerpark, Ledger, Normansville,
>   Penland, Bear Creek, Possum Trot, Rabbit Hop,
>   Liberty Hill, Flat Rock, Minpro, Spruce Pine,
>   Gillespie Gap, McKinney Gap, Hall Town, Dale
>   Road, Creek Town, Sullins Branch, Burleson Hill,
>   Chalk Mountain, Corley Ridge, Humpback
>   Mountain, Altapass, Bad Creek, Beans Creek.

Honey, forgive me for being late!

— R.B. Phillips

The Pasture

I'm going out to clean the pasture spring;
I'll only stop to rake the leaves away
(And wait to watch the water clear, I may):
I shan't be gone long.—You come too.

I'm going out to fetch the little calf
That's standing by the mother. It's so young
It totters when she licks it with her tongue.
I shan't be gone long.—You come too.

— Robert Frost

Abraham Lincoln, Daniel Chester French. Courtesy of Lincoln Memorial.

An honest man is the noblest work of God.
                                    — *James R. Lowell*

CHARACTER

Men of great character have always been in demand and are in a minority. The destiny of all nations depends upon such leadership.

We become what we are by experience and observation of those who precede us. Personal experience alone is too time consuming and expensive.

———•◆◆•►——

Lincoln, the Man of the People

Here was a man to hold against the world,
A man to match the mountains and the sea.
The color of the ground was in him, the red earth;
The smack and tang of elemental things;
The rectitude and patience of the cliff;
The goodwill of the rain that loves all leaves;
The friendly welcome of the wayside well;
The courage of the bird that dares the sea;
The gladness of the wind that shakes the corn;
The pity of the snow that hides all scars;
The secrecy of streams that make their way
Under the mountain to the rifted rock;
The tolerance of equity and light
That gives as freely to the shrinking flower
As to the great oak flaring to the wind—

To the grave's low hill as to the Matterhorn
That shoulders out the sky. Sprung from the West,
He drank the valorous youth of a new world.
The strength of virgin forests braced his mind,
The hush of spacious prairies stilled his soul,
His words were oaks in acorns; and his thoughts
Were roots that firmly gript the granite truth.
And when he fell in whirlwind, he went down
As when a lordly cedar, green with boughs,
Goes down with a great shout upon the hills,
And leaves a lonesome place against the sky.

— *Edwin Markham*

We have many men of science; too few men of God.
We have grasped the mystery of the atom and rejected
    the Sermon on the Mount.
The world has achieved brilliance without wisdom,
    power without conscience.

— *General Omar Bradley*

Early in the Christian experience of Dwight L. Moody, he chanced one day to hear someone make a single statement which presented to him the greatest single challenge of his life. The statement was this: "The world has yet to see what God will do with and for and through and in and by the man who is fully and wholly consecrated to him."

Moody thought: "He did not say a great man, nor a learned man, nor a rich man, nor a wise man, nor an eloquent man, nor a smart man, but simply 'a man.' I am a man, and it lies with a man himself whether he will not make that entire and full consecration. I will try my utmost to be that man."

— *Author unknown*

As a cold-blooded business man, I want to stress my point again. The greatest undeveloped resource is faith. The greatest unused power is prayer. And the coming scientists are going to open these resources and powers. Maybe it won't be in your lifetime, nor in mine. But our grandchildren are going to benefit tremendously when the scientific world starts talking Spiritual Power.

— *Roger Babson*

Sydney Harris once said that the greatest tragedy he knows is for a person to grow from childhood to senility without reaching maturity.

---

1. Is it the truth?
2. Is it fair to all concerned?
3. Will it build good will and better friendship?
4. Will it be beneficial to all concerned?

— *The Four-Way Test of Rotary International*

Within a Man

Goodness doesn't come as a matter of course with good surrounding, and badness doesn't go as a matter of course with bad surroundings. Adam didn't do as well in Eden as Daniel did in Babylon. And when you and I hear it said that good and bad are a simple matter of environment, we know better, whether the man who says so does, or not.

— *Author unknown*

We live by deeds, not years; in thoughts, not breaths; in feelings, not numbers on a dial. We should count time by heart throbs. He lives most who thinks most, feels most, and acts the noblest.

— *Reinhold Niebuhr*

* * *

The Superior Man

I am the inferior of any man whose rights I trample
    underfoot.
Men are not superior by accident of race or color.
They are superior who have the best heart, the best
    brain.
The superior man stands erect by bending over the
    fallen.
He rises by lifting others.

— *Robert Ingersoll*

* * *

Seaworthy

All the water in the world
    However hard it tried,
Could never sink a ship
    Unless it got inside.
All the evil in the world,
    The wickedness and sin,
Can never sink your soul's fair craft
    Unless you let it in.

— *Author unknown*

* * *

The only conquests which are permanent and leave no regrets are our conquests over ourselves.

— *Napoleon Bonaparte*

Mount Rushmore, Gutzon Borglum. Courtesy of National Park Service.

Lives of great men oft remind us
We could make our lives sublime,
And departing, leave behind us,
Footprints on the sands of time.
— *Henry Wadsworth Longfellow*

God Give Us Men

God, give us men! A time like this demands
Great hearts, strong minds, true faith, and willing
    hands;
Men whom the lust of office does not kill;
Men whom the spoils of office cannot buy;
Men who have honor, men who will not lie;
Men who can stand before a demagogue,
And damn his treacherous flatteries without winking!
Tall men, sun-crowned, who will live above the fog
In public duty, and in private thinking:
For while the rabble, with their thumb-worn creeds,
Their large professions, and their little deeds,
Wrangle in selfish strife—lo! Freedom weeps,
Wrong rules the land, and waiting justice sleeps.
— *Joseph G. Holland*

Some Tests for Right and Wrong

The personal test: Will doing it make me a better or worse Christian?

The social test: Will doing it make or influence others to be better or poorer Christians?

The practical test: Will doing it likely bring desirable or undesirable results?

The universal test: Suppose everyone did it?

The scriptural test: Is it expressly forbidden in the word of God?

The stewardship test: Will doing it involve a waste of God's entrustment to me?

The missionary test: Will doing it likely help or hinder the progress of the Kingdom of God?

"He that doubteth is condemned" if he proceeds in the face of his doubts, for "whatsoever is not of faith is sin." (Romans 14:13–23) When in doubt, DON'T.

— *Author unknown*

There is a time in every man's education when he arrives at the conviction that envy is ignorance; that imitation is suicide; that he must take himself for better for worse, as his portion; that though the wide universe is full of good, no kernel of nourishing corn can come to him but through his toil bestowed on that plot of ground which is given to him to till. The power which resides in him is new in nature, and none but he knows what that is which he can do, nor does he know until he has tried.. . . A man is relieved and gay when he has done his best; but what he has said or done otherwise shall give him no peace. . .

Trust thyself: every heart vibrates to that iron string. Accept the place the Divine Providence has found for you, the society of your contemporaries, the connection of events. Great men have always done so. . .

A foolish consistency is the hobgoblin of little minds, adored by little statesmen and philosophers and divines. With consistency a great soul has simply nothing to do. He may as well concern himself with his shadow on the wall. Speak what you think now in hard words; and tomorrow speak what tomorrow thinks in hard words again, though it contradict everything you said today, "Ah, so you shall be sure to be misunderstood."—Is it so bad, then, to be misunderstood? Pythagoras was misunderstood, and Socrates, and Jesus, and Luther, and Copernicus, and Galileo, and Newton, and every pure and wise spirit that ever took flesh. To be great is to be misunderstood.

Greatness appeals to the future. If I can be firm enough today to do right, and scorn eyes, I must have done so much right before as to defend me now. Be it how it will, do right now. Always scorn appearances, and you always may. The force of character is cumulative.

. . . Nothing can bring you peace but yourself. Nothing can bring you peace but the triumph of principles.

— *Ralph Waldo Emerson, (Self-Reliance)*

Four Square

Four things a man must do,
If he would make his record true:
To think without confusion clearly;
To love his fellow man sincerely;
To act from honest motives purely,
And trust in God and heaven securely.
— *Henry Van Dyke*

One Solitary Man

He was born in an obscure village.
He worked in a carpenter shop until he was thirty.
he then became an itinerant preacher.
He never held an office, had a family, or owned a house.
He didn't go to college.
He had no credentials but himself. . .
Nineteen centuries have come and gone, and today
He is the central figure of the human race.
All the armies that ever marched,

Man Carving His Own Destiny, Albin Polvasek.
Courtesy of Brookgreen Gardens.
I am fearfully and wonderfully made.
                    — Psalms 139:14

All the navies that ever sailed,
All the parliaments that ever sat,
And all the kings that ever reigned
Have not affected the life of man
As much as that ONE SOLITARY LIFE.

— *Author unknown*

Lincoln's Ten Guidelines

1. You cannot bring about prosperity by discouraging thrift.
2. You cannot help small men by tearing down big men.
3. You cannot strengthen the weak by weakening the strong.
4. You cannot lift the wage earner by pulling down the wage payer.
5. You cannot help the poor man by destroying the rich.
6. You cannot keep out of trouble by spending more than your income.
7. You cannot further brotherhood of man by inciting class hatred.
8. You cannot establish security on borrowed money.
9. You cannot build character and courage by taking away man's initiative and independence.
10. You cannot help men permanently by doing for them what they could and should do for themselves.

— *Abraham Lincoln*

Man, A Paradox

False of heart, light of ear, bloody of hand;
Hog in sloth, fox in stealth, wolf in greediness, dog in
madness, lion in prey.

— *William Shakespeare, (King Lear)*

. . . And these few precepts in they memory
Look thou character. Give thy thoughts no tongue.
Nor any unproportion'd thought his act.
Be thou familiar, but by no means vulgar.
The friends thou hast, and their adoption tried,
Grapple them to thy soul with hooks of steel:
But do not dull thy palm with entertainment
Of each new-hatch'd, unfledg'd comrade.
Beware of entrance to a quarrel; but, being in,
Bear it, that the opposer may beware of thee.
Give every man thine ear, but few thy voice.
Take each man's censure, but reserve thy judgment.
Costly thy habit, as thy purse can buy,
But not expressed in fancy; rich, not gaudy:
For the apparel oft proclaims the man;
. . . Neither a borrower nor a lender be:
For loan oft loses both itself and friend;
And borrowing dulls the edge of husbandry
This above all,—To thine ownself be true;
And it must follow, as the night the day,
Thou canst not then be false to any man.

— *William Shakespeare, (Hamlet)*

Mystery

"I am fearfully and wonderfully made."*
Contrary to the passionate arrogance of pseudo-
        scientists,
A million years ago the complex chemistry and
        symmetry
Of my body was not a bit different.
How He did it is beyond our ken,
And will be ever so.
However computerized modern laboratories may
        become,

---

*Psalms 139:14

They don't explain the human magnetism of the sexes
Employed to create a fetus;
The warmth and nourishment growing into a child;
The tender care and infinite attention lavished by a
    mother;
The solicitous care of the wife;
The ungrudging labor of the father;
The affection and forethought of the husband.
The home has become so much sweeter
That a new life has come into it.
I am so fearfully and wonderfully made.
I am lovingly shaped by the skillful hands
Of the One who created and revealed the atom.
He took the precious soil of the earth
And molded a creature a little lower than the angels,
And breathed into his nostrils the breath of life;
And he became a living soul.
Then He gave this marvelous creature
The power to have dominion over all He had made.
Ah!, lest we forget, He gave not His handiwork
The power to control himself, except to his own peril.
Man, of all creatures, God chose to guide and fellowship
    with him.
He looked upon His work and pronounced it very good.
He gave him all that does become the measure of a man.
"Here is a man to hold against the world,
To match the mountains and the sea.
The color of the ground was in him, the red earth;
The smack and tang of elemental things.. . . "
Is this the thing the Lord God gave
To have dominion over the sea and the land;
To trace the stars and search the heavens for power;
Is this the dream He dreamed to shape the suns,
And mark their way upon the ancient deep?†
I am so fearfully and wonderfully made.

                           — *R.B. Phillips*

---

†Edwin Markham

What a piece of work is a man! How noble in reason!
How infinite in faculties!
In form and moving, how express and admirable!
In action, how like an angel!
In apprehension how like a god!

— *William Shakespeare, (Hamlet)*

━━◆◆◆━━

*On the day when Albert Schweitzer was to arrive
in Chicago, dignitaries from all walks of society were
on hand to greet him at the train station. When they
located the celebrated physician, concert organist, and
missionary, he was carrying the baggage of an elderly
woman who needed help.*

— *R.B. Phillips*

━━◆◆◆━━

Schweitzer: A Man For The Ages

Amid the clutter of my office stands a fine wood
carving of Albert Schweitzer's head. In the eyes and deep
facial lines the artist captured the spirituality and humility of the 20th century's greatest person.

"Who is that," a student asks, "Albert Einstein?" "No,"
I reply, "a greater man even than Einstein. That is Albert
Schweitzer, of whom Einstein once said, 'There in this
sorry world of ours is a great man.' "

"What was so great about Schweitzer?" the student
wants to know. I explained that to begin with he was one
of those rare geniuses who have more raw talent than ten
ordinary people. "Look at his face," I say, "and imagine a
man who before he was 30 had earned three Ph.D's—in
music, theology, and philosophy. In addition he was Europe's foremost authority on the music of J.S. Bach, and
was in great demand as a concert organist. To that he

added a full-time career as principal of a Theological College and pastor of a church."

By this time my own mind is boggled, if not the student's. Then I informed him that at age 30 Schweitzer, in obedience to a commitment made earlier in life, abruptly resigned all his work and honors to enter medical school to prepare himself to go as a medical doctor to the neediest place he knew on the face of the earth, Equatorial Africa.

"It struck me as incomprehensible that I should be allowed to lead such a happy life, while I saw so many people around me wrestling with care and suffering," he wrote in his autobiography. That one sentence summarizes the life view of Albert Schweitzer, and alone accounts for his incredible career of more than 50 years as a missionary doctor in the most primitive conditions imaginable to the 20th century. He died at age 90 in 1965, a world-renowned figure with a Nobel Peace Prize, important books of philosophy and theology, and numerous honorary degrees to his credit.

— Dr. L.D. Johnson

Len Ganeway Werkner. Brookgreen Gardens. Standing: Bobby E. Phillips and wife, Shirley. Photo by Bobby E. Phillips.

One can live magnificently in this world if one knows how to work and how to love.

— *Leo Tolstoy*

WORK

Somebody asked a famous performer, "How do you get to Lincoln Center?" "Work, work, work" was the reply.

When God created man he instructed him to attend the garden and man has never been his best without work. Such a tragedy to know that many people go through life never learning to love to work. Loving one's work is play—or better.

"One can live magnificently in this world," says Leo Tolstoy, "if he knows how to work and to love, to work for the person one loves and to love one's work."

———

I went by the field of the slothful,
And by the vineyard of the man void of understanding;
And lo, it was all grown over with thorns,
And nettles had covered the face thereof,
And the stone wall thereof was broken down.
Then I saw and considered it well:
I looked upon it and received instructions.
Yet a little sleep, a little slumber
A little folding of the lands to sleep;
So shall thy poverty come as one that travelleth,
And thy want as an armed man.
                    — *Proverbs 24:32–34, arranged by R.B. Phillips*

75

Youth Taming the Wild, Anne Hyatt Huntington.
Courtesy of Brookgreen Gardens.

One machine can do the work of a hundred ordinary men, but no machine can do the work of one extraordinary man.

— *Elbert Hubbard*

The story is told about Albert Einstein, that having finished a paper, he looked about for a paper clip. The one he found in the drawer was too badly bent for use. While looking about for a tool to straighten it he found a whole box of unused clips. Immediately he started to shape one of them into a tool to straighten the bent one. When asked why he was doing this when he had a full box of new ones, he replied, "I formed a habit early in life that once I undertook a task never to leave it unfinished."

— *R.B. Phillips*

My Answer

I am a teenager. How can I convince my dad that modern kids shouldn't do hard work?

You poor, deluded adolescent! You ought to be ashamed to eat your dad's food, sleep in his beds, ride in his car, and then shirk your home responsibility. I think you have put your finger on one of the younger generation's weaknesses. Luckily, not all boys are as lazy and conniving as you are. But too many think of life as a colossal picnic, planned for their ease and enjoyment. Honest work never hurt anyone. There is nothing disgraceful about working with your hands. Jesus was a carpenter, Paul a tent-maker, and Peter a fisherman. They became great because they took their share of responsibility in the meager tasks of life, and when the bigger challenges came they were prepared to meet them. The world of the future needs ambitious, enterprising men. It will be a sort of a "survival of the fittest" proposition. If you dodge even the little responsibilities, I fear that if there are many of your stamp, the future will not be much to look forward to. Wake up and stop shirking. You and those around you will be much happier.

— *Billy Graham*

[Work is] that blessed yoke without which we cannot live.

— *Sir Laurence Olivier*

I know of no greater blessing a person could experience than to find useful work that is both challenging and satisfying. Such a person has little or no need for play. Thomas Edison said he saw no need for a vacation, since he got more satisfaction from his work. What greater joy could one anticipate than that experienced by a sculptor who said of one of his works: "I have not wrought it for money;. . . a well spring of wisdom gushed within me as I wrought upon the oak with my whole strength, and soul, and faith."

— *R.B. Phillips*

There is a legend at Harvard to the effect that the late Le Baron Russel Briggs, long the beloved dean of the college, once asked a student why he had failed to complete an assignment.

"I wasn't feeling very well, sir," said the student.

"Mr. Smith," said the dean, "I think that in time you may perhaps find that most of the work of the world is done by people who aren't feeling very well."

Thank God every morning when you get up that you have something to do that day which must be done, whether you like it or not.

— *Charles Kingsley*

In Memory of the Workhorse, Anne Hyatt Huntington. Courtesy of Brookgreen Gardens. Photo:
Bobby Phillips

"How do you get to Lincoln Center?"
"Work, work, work," replied the performer.
— *Author unknown*

River Driver, Charles Eugene Tefft. Courtesy of
Brookgreen Gardens.

Stormy, husky, brawling,. . . bareheaded, shovel-
ing, wrecking, planning, building, breaking,
rebuilding. . .

— *Carl Sandburg*

Chicago

Hog Butcher for the World,
Tool Maker, Stacker of Wheat,
Player with Railroads and the Nation's Freight Handler;
Stormy husky, brawling,
City of the Big Shoulders:

They tell me you are wicked and I believe them, for I
    have seen your painted women under the gas lamp
    luring the farm boys.
And they tell me you are crooked, and I answer: Yes, it
    is true I have seen the gunman kill and go free to
    kill again.
And they tell me you are brutal and my reply is: On the
    faces of women and children I have seen the marks
    of wanton hunger.
And having answered so, I turn once more to those who
    sneer at this my city, and I give them back the sneer
    and say to them:
Come and show me another city with lifted head singing
    so proud to be alive and coarse and strong and
    cunning.
Flinging magnetic curses amid the toil of piling job on
    job, here is a tall bold slugger set vivid against the
    little soft cities;
Fierce as a dog with tongue lapping for action, cunning
    as a savage pitted against the wilderness,
    Bareheaded,
    Shoveling,
    Wrecking,
    Planning,
    Building, breaking, rebuilding.
Under the smoke, dust all over his mouth, laughing with
    white teeth,
Under the terrible burden of destiny laughing as a
    young man laughs,
Laughing even as an ignorant fighter laughs who has
    never lost a battle,

Bragging and laughing that under his wrist is the pulse,
  and under his ribs the heart of the people,
  Laughing!
Laughing the stormy, husky, brawling laughter of Youth,
  half-naked, sweating, proud to be Hog Butcher,
  Tool-Maker, Staker of Wheat, Player
With Railroads, and Freight Handler to the Nation.
— *Carl Sandburg*

Definitions of Genius

"Before I was a genius, I was a drudge."
— *Paderewski*
"If people knew how hard I work to get my mastery
it wouldn't seem so wonderful after all."
— *Michelangelo*
"Genius is the capacity for taking infinite pains."
— *Carlyle*
"All the genius I have is merely the fruit of labor."
— *Alexander Hamilton*

. . . A much-maligned term today is what binds a
person to himself, and a community or civilization together . . . Approach work with discipline and imagination—the discipline which leads people to choose
whether to spend their time shoddily or well. Imagination
releases us from the prison of ourselves, and is not an
escape, but a plunge into the reality around us.
— *Wilma Dryman in an address at Lees-McRae College,*
May 10, 1986

Two Ways

No line of work is interesting or uninteresting in itself. There are two different approaches to each task. Much depends upon the amount of thought, ingenuity, and effort put into it, but much more depends on the mental attitude. Our job, whether it be junkman or judge, is very much what we make it.

The following parallel statements show how a task can be made easy or hard; a joy or drudge:

"I am a housewife, and without question I have the most uninteresting job in the world. My life is the same year in and year out—dishwashing, sweeping, and dusting. It's not such hard work. I can finish it in a few hours each day—then I am bored with myself, my friends, and my family the rest of the day. I wish I had an interesting job where I could meet people, exciting people who are really doing things. An ever-changing job which would keep me absorbed every minute."

"I am a housewife, and without question I have the most interesting job in the world. My days are full of planning new things for our home, clever ways of making it more attractive for my family and my friends. See that furniture over there? I painted and decorated it myself. My only complaint about my job is that the days are much too short to accomplish everything I planned. My time is my own—I wouldn't trade positions with anyone."

— *Author unknown*

Albert Schweitzer wrote from his hospital in the the heart of Africa:

"What do all these difficulties count for compared with the joy of being here, working and helping? Just to see the joy of those who are plagued with sores, when these have been cleanly bandaged up and they no longer have to drag their poor, bleeding feet through the mud, makes it worthwhile to work here."

It's a good thing our forefathers didn't have Guaranteed Income. There would have been no America.

The immigrants (from whom all of us descended) had no income, only ambition. So they sold what little they had, borrowed the rest, and came here by miserable steerage, for a chance to work.

No job was too menial; they took it, and did it well. They didn't demand "fringe benefits" nor high wages, and if there wasn't a job they created one.

Italians who couldn't even speak the language pushed carts, weary miles a day, selling whatever they could. Irish dug ditches. Germans ran tiny shops, English mined coal. People of these and many other nationalities worked so hard they didn't have time to complain—they just built this nation and their own self-respecting future.

You and I don't deserve a home. We don't deserve so-and-so much income. We don't deserve security. We only deserve the chance to try to earn these things for ourselves.

Most Americans want work; our interest and effort should be directed toward helping them get it, helping them prepare for it. But there are some who make a profession of poverty—people who won't work, and who don't intend to work as long as they can get "welfare." They say it is "society's fault" they are poor, when actually it is more apt to be their own laziness.

Ambition to work doesn't cost anything, but it solves more problems.

Abraham Lincoln said: "You cannot build character and courage by taking away men's initiative and independence. You cannot help men permanently by doing for them what they could do for themselves."

— *Warner & Swasey, U.S. News*

―・◆・◆・■―

Blessed is he who has found his work;
let him ask no other blessedness.
— *Thomas Carlyle*

I am glad to think
I am not bound to make the world go right,
But only to discover and to do
With cheerful heart the work that God appoints.

— *Joan Ingelow*

Hands. My husband's hands. I think often of those hands of his. They are always busy for those dear to him. . . .

My husband seems challenged to do everything with his hands right and good.

Sometimes his hands are busy pitching a ball to our son or helping to fly a kite.

At times they are stern hands, administering a spanking, and the children don't like it because he spanks hard enough to carry the lesson home. As I said, he does things well with his hands.

These hands are a bit rough, but I love them. At night, after a busy day, we like to sit awhile and watch our favorite TV programs. Our chairs are side by side, thanks to a small house—which has its advantages after all. As he watches, he reaches over and takes my hand in his.

Often I think of those hands and the thousands of things they have found to do. Silently I thank God for my husband's hands.

— *Cozette Holmes Mott*

For we hear that there are some which walk among you disorderly, working not at all, but are busybodies.

Now them that are such we command and exhort by our Lord Jesus Christ, that with quietness they work, and eat their own bread . . . if any would not work, neither should he eat.

— *II Thessalonians 3:10–12*

Make soft living and you make soft men. Put clothes on the savage and he catches cold. Domesticate fowl and they roost low where something gets them. Coddle youngsters and they whine. Give a boy a business and his creditors close in next year.

The only man who can keep his feet without something to lean on is the man who had strength enough to get to his feet unaided. While working his way to the top, a man develops the ability to hold his place when he gets there.

Neither nations nor individuals can stand prosperity. They get soft; they lose character; they develop the vices of the bored.

As a people we can't save ourselves by disposing of our riches and returning to primitive ways; but just as the office man takes exercises as a substitute for plowing, so parents may create hardships and require the youngsters to earn their spending money though the family purse is overflowing.

To "give the kid an easier time than you had" is to keep him in the Tropics where the monkey has made no advance.

— *Robert Quillen*

The Necessity For Work

Men of God have always been hard workers. Work can bring, not only health to our bodies, but peace to our minds and the consciousness of helping to build the kingdom of God.

I read somewhere that the body of every organization is structured with four kinds of bones. There are the wishbones, who spend all their time wishing that someone else would do the work. Then there are the jawbones who do all the talking but little else. The knucklebones, who knock anything anybody else tries to do. Fortunately, in every organization there are the backbones, who get under the load and do most of the work. — *Claude Frazier*

"If I omit practice one day, I notice it; if two days, my friends notice it; if three, the public notices it."

— Rubenstein, the great musician

When Earth's Last Picture Is Painted

When Earth's last picture is painted and the tubes are
    twisted and dried,
When the oldest colours have faded, and the youngest
    critic has died,
We shall rest, and faith, we shall need it—lie down for
    an aeon or two,
Till the Master of All Good Workmen shall put us to
    work anew.

And those that were good shall be happy: they shall sit
    in a golden chair;
They shall splash at a ten-league canvas with brushes of
    comet's hair.
They shall find real saints to draw from—Magdalene,
    Peter, and Paul;
They shall work for an age at a sitting and never be tired
    at all!

And only the Master shall praise us, and only the Master
    shall blame;
And no one shall work for money, and no one shall work
    for fame,
But each for the joy of the working, and each, in his
    separate star,
Shall draw the Thing as he sees It for the God of Things
    as They are!

— Rudyard Kipling

Mother and Child, William Zorach.

For fear of losing you I hold you tight to my breast.

— *Rabindranath Tagore*

MOTHERHOOD

Perhaps it is a trite saying that the future of civilization is largely determined by the type of mothers we have. The father's influence on children is far less. The mother's influence is felt on a child perhaps even before its birth.

Mama, Mama

"Ah, she's gone—or is she?"
She asks—a three-year-old—of hers and mine.
"Some things we're not yet to know, my child!
But this we know—not all—
Enough to know she's seen His face,
And in His presence lives forever;
And love she knows as no other earthly one has known.

She dwells with joy, and peace, and mercy, and truth;
She drinks her fill of sweetest music sung by heavenly
        choirs—
No sorrow, no pain, no fear, no death!"
"Mama, Mama! does she hear me, Daddy?
—Yes I see her; she smiles and reaches for me!
O take me to you, Mama;
This world is so cruel and unkind!"

— R.B. Phillips

The Beginning

"Where have I come from, where did you pick me up?" the baby asked its mother. She, half crying, half laughing, and clasping the baby to her breast: "You were hidden in my heart as its desire, my darling.

"You were in the dolls of my childhood's games; and then with clay I made the image of my god each morning. I made and unmade you then.

"You were enshrined in our household deity, I worshipped you.

"In all my hopes and loves, in my life, in the life of my mother, I lived.

"In the lap of the deathless spirit who rules our home you have been nursed for ages.

"When in girlhood my heart was opening its petals, you hovered as a fragrance about it.

Joy of Motherhood, Hirsch. Courtesy of Brookgreen Gardens.
Photo: Bobby Phillips

Where have I come from, where did you pick me up?
— *Rabindranath Tagore*

"Your tender softness bloomed in my youthful limbs, like a glow in the sky before the sunrise.

"Heaven's first darling, twin born with the morning light, you have floated down the stream of the world's life, and at last you have stranded in my heart.

"As I gaze on your face, mystery overwhelms me: you who belong to all have become mine.

"For fear of losing you I hold you tight to my breast. What magic has snared the world's treasure in the slender arms of mine?"

— *Rabindranath Tagore, (The Crescent Moon)*

A Boy's Mother

My mother she's so good to me
If I was good as I could be,
I couldn't be as good—no sir!
Can't any boy be good as her!

She loves me when I'm glad er sad;
She loves me when I'm good er bad;
An' what's a funniest thing, she says
She loves me when she punishes.

I don't like her to punish me—
That don't hurt, but it hurts to see
Her cryin'—Nen I cry; an' nen
We both cry an' be good again.

She loves me when she cuts and sews
My little clock an' Sunday clothes;
An' when my Pa comes home to tea;
She loves him most as much as me.

She laughs an' tells him all I said,
An' grabs me up an' pats my head;
An' I hug her an' hug my Pa
An' love him purt'nigh much as Ma.

— *Author unknown*

Of The World's 'Meanest Mother'
And Her Legacy

A woman recalled the painful years when she was growing up. She said, "As a child I had the meanest mother in the whole world. She was real mean. When other kids ate candy for breakfast, she made me eat cereal, eggs, and toast. When others had cake and candy

Pioneer Woman, Bryant Baker.

> . . . But all in front of me is untilled land,
> The wilderness and solitary place.
> — *Author unknown*

for lunch, I had to eat a sandwich. As you can guess, my dinner was different from other kids'.

"My mother insisted on knowing where we were at all times. You'd think we were on a chain gang. She had to know who our friends were and what we were doing. She insisted that if we said we'd be gone for an hour, that we would be gone one hour or less. She was real mean.

"I am ashamed to admit it, but she actually had the nerve to break the child labor law. She made us work! We had to wash all the dishes, make beds, learn to cook, and all sorts of cruel things. I believe she lay awake at nights thinking up mean things to do to us.

"She always insisted on us telling the truth, the whole truth and nothing but the truth. By the time we were teenagers she was much wiser, and our life became even more unbearable.

"None of this tooting the horn of a car for us to come running. She embarrassed us no end by making our dates and friends come to the door to get us. I forgot to mention, while my friends were dating at the mature age of 12 or 13, my old-fashioned mother refused to let me date until I was 15 or 16.

"My mother was a complete failure as a mother. None of us has ever been arrested, or beaten a mate. Each of my brothers served his time in the service of his country. And whom do we have to blame for this terrible way we turned out? You're right, our mean mother.

"Look at all things we missed. We never got to take part in a riot, burn draft cards, and a million and one things that our friends did. She made us grow up into God-fearing, educated honest adults.

"Using this as a background, I am trying to raise my children. I stand a little taller and I am filled with pride when my children call me mean. You see, I thank God He gave me the meanest mother in the world."

From this, we would say the country doesn't need a five-cent cigar; it needs more "mean" mothers . . . and dads.   — *Author unknown*

Madonna of Trail, Artist unknown.

The queen that bore thee oftener upon her knees
  than on her feet,
Died every day she lived.
                    — *William Shakespeare, (Macbeth)*

A Mother's Prayer

My son left today, Lord, and with him went a part of me. Nothing seems quite finished; there's an emptiness in me aching to be filled.

With a suitcase in each hand, he left smiling. It felt so great to him to be on his own. Lord, help me to remember my first days of independence and to realize how very necessary they are.

Well, Lord, I can't see that he is comfortable tonight, all tucked in under warm, handmade quilts. So God, I'm believing that you will see to that for me. I pray too that he will have something warm and nourishing to eat.

My arms ache, Lord, to hold him close once more. (He will always be my little boy, my baby.) But I'm not there, so you must encircle him with your eternal perfect love. Please send others to love him and show him kindness.

When decision time comes his way, I won't be there, so please Lord, give him wisdom and insight and see him through.

When he fails, I won't be around to console and encourage; but Lord, let him feel your presence then. I pray that he will know that his strength and power to try again comes from you.

When my son is lonely, I cannot be by his side; but I pray that you will make yourself greatly known to him in those secluded moments. I pray that he will recognize the beauty of intimacy with you, God.

When he needs to talk to a friend, I ask you to lead in the conversation. Comfort and direct him; place persons in his pathway to whom he can relate. Show him the reason to live and then strengthen him to live for that reason.

When he is happy, God, I pray you will release his jubilant spirit and let him rejoice in Life's richness. Give him someone who will laugh with him and share happiness.

When he is sick, Lord, and I can't be there to care for him, I'm countin' on you, the Great Physician, to be ever at his side. What more can a mama do than to release her babies into your omnipotent care. . .

Well, Goodnight, Lord; I'll talk with you again in the morning. Thank you for being with my son and doing all these things for him while we're apart.. . . Come to think of it, Lord, you are really the One who met all of his needs even when we were together.

I love you, God. Amen.

— *Joyce Boone*

My Kitchen

Lord of all pots, and pans, and things;
Since I've not time to be a saint by doing lovely things,
Or watching late with Thee,
Or dreaming in the dawn of light,
Or storming heaven's gates,
Make me a saint by getting meals,
And washing up the plates.

Warm all the kitchen with Thy love,
And light it with Thy peace;
Forgive me all my worry,
And make my grumbling cease.
Thou who didst love to give men food,
In room or by the sea,
Accept this service that I do;
I do it unto Thee.

— *Author unknown*

The Windy Doorstep, S.L. Eberle. Courtesy of Brookgreen Gardens. Photo: Bobby Phillips

While I must work because I am old,
And the seed of fire gets feeble and cold.
— *William Butler Yeats*

The Christ Child, Labram Belskie. Courtesy of
Brookgreen Gardens.

Unto us a child is born.
— *Isaiah 9:6*

MORAL CRISIS

Arnold Toynbee, the great British historian, tells us that of the 21 great civilizations he studied, 18 fell in the same manner.

When Daniel Webster was asked to forecast the future of America, he indicated (1) abundance, (2) luxury, (3) decline, (4) desolation. This appraisal has been confirmed by Toynbee and many other wise men through the ages.

Lest we despair, the human race is resilient and in the long run seems to learn from the past. Theodore Roosevelt may have said it well 75 years ago: "We see across the dangers the great future, and we rejoice as a giant refreshed . . . The great victories are yet to be won, the greatest deeds yet to be done."

Let us hope and pray that the leadership of our great country will learn the lessons from history and thus avoid catastrophe.

If we ever pass out as a great nation, we ought to put on our tombstone: "America died from the delusion that she had moral leadership."

— *Will Rogers*

In 1787 Gibbon completed his notable work, The Decline and Fall of the Roman Empire. Here is the way he accounted for its fall:

1. The rapid increase of divorce; the undermining of the dignity and sanctity of the home.
2. Higher and higher taxes and the spending of monies for free bread and circuses for the populace.
3. The mad craze for pleasure; sports becoming every year more exciting and more brutal.
4. The building of gigantic armaments when the real enemy was within, in the decadence of the people.

It is not difficult to see all these characteristics in our own country. There are certain other signs of decay in our society:

1. Materialism. With the unprecedented development of technology, too many people have come to believe the fallacious idea that the accumulation of things is all important, and that nothing else matters.

2. Loss of satisfaction in craftsmanship and the joy of accomplishment. The development of the assembly line in industry has magnified this problem. Several other countries are producing better products with more production per man-hour and at lower wages.

3. Craze to be entertained. It is no exaggeration to say that much of our entertainment is a total waste of time. The news media might lead one to believe that our schools and colleges are designed mostly for playing games. We do not seem to have time to think, meditate, listen to good music, read, paint, write, take a walk, or carry on an intelligent conversation. While visiting Bok Gardens in Lake Wales, Florida, I noted where John Burrows had said: "It's so easy to lose ourselves in this world. I come here often to try to find myself." It is well known that there is an increasing amount of dissipation, drugs, alcohol drinking, smoking, pornography, and venereal disease.

4. The decay of real worship of God. As our churches become larger, more affluent and powerful, they tend to forget the purpose for which they were formed, drift into formality, and feel sufficient unto them-selves. I realize that this statement is debatable to many people, but I am convinced that mankind is evil by nature. A newborn infant will always be selfish until somebody or circumstances teaches him better.

5. Corruption in high places. Most people have lost confidence in their governmental leadership. The government seems to be operated for the benefit of the pressure groups and a swarm of bureaucrats. Elected officials were once considered servants of the people, but not it appears that an individual finds it nearly impossible to get an effective hearing. People with power seldom give it up until they have to. Those without power do not get it until the powerful get too weak, through dissipation and corruption, to defend themselves.

A country does not grow great by finding which way the people are headed and getting in front of them. A statesman studies the need of his people, develops worthwhile ideas, and sets about to sell the ideas to the people. He should visualize what people need instead of always trying to give them what the power structure wants.

If we do not learn from history, we are destined to repeat it.

— R.B. Phillips

Our Father Who Art In Heaven

We pray that you save us from ourselves. The world that you have made for us, to live in peace, we have made into an armed camp. We live in fear of war to come. We are afraid of "the terror that flies by night and the arrow that flies by day, the pestilence that walks in darkness and the destruction that wastes at noon-day."

We have turned from You to go our selfish way; we have broken your commandments and denied your truth.

We have left Your altars to serve the false gods of money and pleasure and power. Forgive us and help us.

Now, darkness gathers around us and we are confused in all our counsels, losing faith in You we lose in ourselves. Inspire us with wisdom, all of us of every color, race and creed, to use our wealth, our strength to help our brother, instead of destroying him. Help us to do your will as it is done in heaven and be worthy of your promise of peace on earth. Fill us with new faith, new strength, and new courage, that we may win the Battle for Peace.

Be swift to save us, dear God, before the darkness falls. Amen.

— *U.S. News*

Man Has Changed—God Hasn't

Man has changed again and again, but the mandates from God are still the same as they have always been because the fundamental principles of good behavior are immutable.

"In all these (religions), the feeling is prominent that the human being is under the ever-present influence of Something, is always in relation with Something, which is other than what is perceptible to the outer senses; that the life of the physical body is subordinate to the life of a Mysterious Something, the Soul, the Spirit, which has a life beyond this life."

To achieve this emancipation from the shackles of modern ideologies, we must grow a Christmas tree that doesn't wither the day after Christmas—a tree that is nourished within our own hearts and spreads its branches from man to man as it unites us all in a world of eternal love.

— *David Lawrence, (U.S. News), 1955*

Mares of Diomedes, Gutzon Borglum. Courtesy of Brookgreen
Gardens.

Lord God of Hosts, be with us yet,
Lest we forget—lest we forget!
— *Rudyard Kipling*

Woe unto them that rise up early in the morning,
That they may follow strong drink;
That continue until night; till wine inflame them!
And the harp, and the viol, the tabret,
And pipe, and wine, are in their feasts:
But they regard not the work of the Lord,
Neither consider the operation of His hands.
Therefore my people are gone into captivity,
Because they have no knowledge:
And their honorable men are famished
And their multitude dried up with thirst.. . .
Woe unto them that are mighty to drink wine,
And men of strength to mingle strong drink.. . .
— *Isaiah 5:11–13,22*

Woe unto him that giveth his neighbor drink, that putteth thy bottle to him, and maketh him drunken also, that thou mayest look on their nakedness!

— *Habakkuk 2:15*

<hr />

Ike Asks: Is Morality Declining?

"What has happened to our concept of beauty and decency and morality?"

Former President Dwight Eisenhower asked that question of Americans. In a speech at the dedication ceremonies for the Eisenhower Presidential Library in Abilene, Kansas, he gave his views on some facets of modern America.

"We venerate the pioneers. . . their sturdiness, their self-reliance, their faith in their God. . . . Now, I wonder if some of those people could come back today and see us doing the twist instead of the minuet—whether they would be particularly struck by the beauty of that dance?

". . . We see movies and the stage, and books and periodicals using vulgarity, sensuality, indeed, downright filth to sell their wares. . . . We see our very art forms so changed that (some modern art). . . looks as if a broken-down tin lizzie loaded with paint has driven over it."

The 72-year-old former war hero and ex-President sees some hope, however. "Now, America today is just as strong as it needs to be," he said. "America is the strongest nation in the world, and she will never be defeated or damaged seriously by anyone from the outside. Only Americans can ever hurt us.

". . . I am confident that the American people will see to it that our spiritual strength, that the morale of this country is just as strong . . . as it was in the days of Lincoln or Washington or the others."

— *U.S. News*

I could be wrong, and hope I am wrong, but it seems to me that our nation is in bad shape psychologically and spiritually if it needs to venerate a movie star, however charismatic his image, more than any other national figure of our day. The hyperdulia heaped upon him after his death does not dismay me—people have a right to enshrine anyone they want to—as much as the fact that no political figure, no educator, no scientist or sage or moral leader, comes anywhere near commanding such breadth of identity, devotion, or esteem. This may say more about us than it does about him.

— Sidney J. Harris

The poorer citizens have captured the government and have voted the property of the rich into the coffers of the state for redistribution among the voters.

Politicians have strained their ingenuity to discover new sources of public revenue. They have doubled the indirect taxes, such as customs due on imports and exports. They have continued the extraordinary taxes of wartime into peacetime. They have broadened perilously the field of the income tax as well as the property tax.

One of our wisest says, "When I was a boy, wealth was regarded as secure and admirable. . . but now a man has to defend himself for being rich, as if it were the worst of crimes."

Athletics have become professionalized; young citizens who once thronged the playgrounds of the gymnasium now exert themselves vicariously by witnessing professional exhibitions.

Philosophy has struggled to find in civic loyalty or in a national ethic some substitute for the divine commandments and the surveillance of God.

— Socrates, 363 B.C.

When Fiorello La Guardia was mayor of New York City, he hung above his desk at City Hall this pronouncement by Abraham Lincoln:

"If I were to try to read, much less answer, all the attacks made on me, this shop might as well be closed for any other business. I do the very best I know how, the very best I can, and I mean to keep doing so until the end. If the end brings me out all right, what is said against me won't amount to anything. If the end brings me out wrong, 10 angels swearing I was right would make no difference."

— *Arthur H. Prince*

A Modern Fable

"Train up a child in the way he should go." —Proverbs 22:6.

Once there was a little boy. When he was three weeks old his parents turned him over to a baby sitter. When he was two they dressed him up like a cowboy and gave him a gun. When he was three everybody said, "How cute," as he went lisping a beer commercial jingle.

When he was six, his father occasionally dropped him off at Sunday School on his way to the golf course. When he was eight they bought him a BB gun and taught him to shoot sparrows. He learned to shoot windshields himself.

When he was ten he spent his afternoon time squatting at the drug store news stand reading comic books. His mother wasn't home and his father was busy.

When he was 13, he told his parents other boys stayed out as late as they wanted to so they said he could, too. It was easier that way.

When he was 14 they gave him a deadly two-ton machine, wrangled a license for him to drive it, and told him to be careful.

When he was 15, the police called his home one night and said "We have your boy. He's in trouble."

"In trouble!" screamed the father. "It can't be my boy!" But it was.

— *Author unknown*

Our Changing Characteristics

Change is the inexorable law of all things temporal. Too often, however, when we discuss changes, the emphasis is laid almost entirely on things material. James Truslow Adams, one of the best essayists in America today, in an article in "The Forum," takes up what is much more important—our changing characteristics. As quoted in the Raleigh News and Observer, Mr. Adams summarizes certain of these changes, as follows:

1. We are substituting self-expression for self-discipline.
2. We are substituting the idea of prosperity for the idea of liberty.
3. We are substituting the mood of restlessness for the mood of rest.
4. We are substituting a philosophy of spending for a philosophy of saving.
5. We are substituting show for solidity.
6. We are substituting desire for the new and untried, for affection for the old and the tried.
7. We are substituting dependence for self-reliance.
8. We are substituting gregariousness for solitude.
9. We are substituting luxury for simplicity.
10. We are substituting ostentation for restraint.
11. We are substituting the pursuit of success for the passion of integrity.
12. We are substituting nationalism for localism.
13. We are substituting easy generosity for wise giving.
14. We are substituting a preference for impressions for a preference for thought.

15. We are substituting democratic preferences for aristocratic preferences.
16. We are substituting facts for ideas.
17. We are substituting the mediocre for the excellent.

This is a serious picture which Mr. Adams presents. An hour or so of Sunday calm might well be devoted to a consideration of the substitutions which are in progress.

Someday the spirit of Christmas will mean more in national and international affairs than it does today.

Someday there will be peace on earth.

Someday there will be good will toward men.

When?

Can it be while men hate each other, deceive one another, envy one another, rob one another?

Can it be while men, without basis, question each other's integrity instead of debating issues and ideas?

Can it be while those who boast of freedom and democracy are intolerant of the views of others in their own communities and really do not believe in freedom of speech for their fellowmen?

Can it be while men malign one another and distort truth just to win an election to public office?

Can it be while men in foreign lands conspire to enslave their fellow men—to imprison them in isolated camps far from their homes and families?

Can it be while tyrants deny liberty to the individual and wield the scepters of despotism over millions of helpless persons?

Can it be while men who profess to be righteous sit down to bargain with evil regimes and to negotiate a "live and let live" philosophy that openly condones sin and cravenly runs away from the sacrifices so necessary to win a triumph for a cause that is just?

Can it be while men surrender principle and morality and excuse their conduct as necessary to meet "political expediency" in international relations?

Can it be while we prate of morals and idealism, and then sell our souls amid the hypocrisies of the hour?

The world each year is reminded of Christmas in an outburst of generosity toward kinfolk and friends. But the gifts mostly are of material things. The voice of the spiritual is rarely heard above the din of the crowd. We recite the rituals, but do we fulfill the words which speak the true creed?

———•◦◆◦•———

This is an age of decaying morals and of crass materialism. The prophets of old have been silenced. The new prophets urge the advantages of compromise with evil—they terrorize the people with a strange fear of death. They regard sacrifice as obsolete. Jesus, they argue in effect, would better have appeased the enemy.

The motivation to resist tyrannical masters at the risk of death has always been heroic, but nowadays we are asked to buy security at any price—even at the price of ideals and moral principle.

The Great Martyrs of all times had no fear of mortal death. His was to the last a voice of patience and restraint, of charity and forgiveness. There was no flinching in the test.

We speak of peace as an objective, but we seldom examine the ingredients of peace that compromise the moral force of mankind.

For until the spirit that permeated the life and teachings of Jesus nearly two thousand years ago becomes the code of mankind, there will be continuous friction and misunderstanding and perhaps even war.

People do not willingly fight one another. Rulers bring on war by misleading oppressed peoples, hiding the truth from them and falsely accusing other nations of threatening attack. It is the oldest crime in all history. We are conscious of its vicious impact today. Only truth can overcome it by reaching into the hearts of men everywhere.

Someday there will be a real Christmas. Someday the peoples of the world will rise to pay homage to the principles that will assure peace.

But the real Christmas will never come through the electric display of slogans or the myriads of tinseled trees exhibited along our thoroughfares.

The real Christmas will come when men have discovered within themselves the power that overnight can frustrate any commands issued by the despots.

The real Christmas will come when, among nations like our own and our allies, there is an impulse to follow the courageous will of a liberated Conscience.

To achieve this emancipation from the shackles of modern ideologies, we must grow a Christmas tree that doesn't wither the day after Christmas—a tree that is nourished within our own hearts and spreads its branches from man to man as it unites us all in a world of eternal love.

— *David Lawrence, (U.S. News), 1955*

Recessional

God of our Fathers, known of old,
    Lord of our far-flung battle-line,
Beneath whose awful Hand we hold
    Dominion over palm and pine—
Lord God of Hosts, be with us yet,
Lest we forget—lest we forget!

The tumult and the shouting dies;
    The Captains and the Kings depart:
Still stands Thine ancient sacrifice,
    An humble and a contrite heart.
Lord God of Hosts, be with us yet,
Lest we forget—Lest we forget!

Far-called, our navies melt away;
 On dune and headland sinks the fire:
Lo, all our pomp of yesterday
 Is one with Nineveh and Tyre!
Judge of the Nations, spare us yet,
Lest we forget—Lest we forget!

If, drunk with sight power, we loose
 Wild tongues that have not Thee in awe,
Such boasting as the Gentiles use
 Or lesser breeds without the Law—
Lord God of Hosts, be with us yet,
Lest we forget—Lest we forget!

For heathen heart that puts her trust
 In reeking tube and iron shard,
All valiant dust that builds on dust,
 And guarding calls not Thee to guard,
For frantic boast and foolish word—
The Mercy on Thy People, Lord!
     — *Rudyard Kipling*

———

 Wine is a mocker, strong drink is raging: and whosoever is deceived thereby is not wise.
     — *Proverbs 20:1*

———

 Be not among wine bibers;
Among riotous eaters of flesh:
For the drunkard and the glutton
Shall come to poverty:
And drowsiness shall clothe a man with rage.
— *Proverbs 23:20–21, arranged by R.B. Phillips*

Many years ago a wise philosopher came to this country seeking the answer to the question: wherein lies the greatness and genius of America? This was his answer:

I sought for the greatness and genius of America in her commodious harbors and her ample rivers—and it was not there.

I sought in her fertile fields and boundless forest— in her rich mines and vast world commerce—and it was not there.

I sought for the greatness and genius of America in her democratic Congress and her matchless Constitution—it was not there.

Not until I went into the churches of America and heard her pulpits flame with righteousness did I understand the secret of her genius and power.

America is great because America is good—and if America ever ceases to be good, America will cease to be great.

— Author unknown

All that is necessary for the triumph of evil is that enough good men do nothing.

— Author unknown

Cowards die many times before their death;
The valiant never taste of death but once.
Of all the wonders that I yet have heard,
It seems to me more strange that man should fear,
Seeing that death, a necessary end,
Will come when it will come.

— William Shakespeare, (Julius Caesar)

There was a dream. . . that men could one day speak the thoughts of their own choosing.—There was a hope . . . that men could one day stroll through streets at evening, unafraid.—There was a prayer. . . that each could speak to his own God—in his own church—That dream, that hope, that prayer became. . . America!—Now great strength, youthful heart, vast enterprise, hard work make it so.—Now that same America is the dream. . . the hope . . . the prayer of the world. Our freedom—its dream. Our strength—its hope. Our swift race against time—its prayer! We must not fail the world now. We must not fail to share our freedom afterwards.. . .

— *Author unknown*

A Mill Boy, Photographer unknown.
Mammon is the largest slaveholder in the world.
— *Frederick Saunders*

WEALTH and POVERTY

All history is filled with the problem of unequal distribution of wealth. It records a few living in great luxury while others lived in unspeakable poverty.

This fact does not necessarily indicate that all rich are selfish and oppressive while all poor are great. Too many factors enter into this problem to attempt to simplify it. Some are born into homes where they are inspired, motivated, and stirred with ambition. Many lack these advantages and their lives reflect this deprivation. Society has not yet solved this problem but let's hope the law of the jungle which, in the name of "free enterprise," permits the strong to piteously exploit the weak will not endure. History teaches us that to continue this policy ends in violence.

Who steals my purse steals trash
'Twas mine, 'tis his, and has been slave to thousands;
But he who filches from me my good name
Robs me of that which enriches not him,
And makes me poor indeed.

— *William Shakespeare*

Not what we give but what we share
For the gift without the giver is bare;
Who gives himself with his alms feeds three—
Himself, his hungering neighbor, and me.

— *James Russell Lowell*

There is a destiny that makes us brothers;
None goes his way alone:
All that we send into the lives of others
Comes back into our own.

— *Edwin Markham*

Because thou sayest, I am rich, and increased with
goods, and have need of nothing; and knowest not that
thou art wretched, and miserable, and poor, and blind,
and naked.

— *Revelation 3:17*

Elegy Written In A Country Churchyard

The curfew tolls the knell of parting day,
    The lowing herd wind slowly o'er the lea,
The plowman homeward plods his weary way,
    And leaves the world to darkness and to me.. . .

The boast of heraldry, the pomp of power,
    And all that beauty, all that wealth e'er gave,
Awaits alike th' inevitable hour.
    The paths of glory lead but to the grave.. . .

Full many a gem of purest ray serene
    The dark, unfathomed caves of ocean bear;
Full many a flower is born to blush unseen,
    And waste its sweetness on the desert air.. . .

— *Thomas Gray*

What Are Wise Men Saying Now About Money?

Greatest god below the sky.   —Spencer
The almighty dollar!   —Washington Irving
Put not your trust in money, but put your money in trust.
                                                      —Holmes
What's money without happiness?   —Bulwer-Lytton
The wretched impotence of gold.   —Young
Mammon is the largest slaveholder in the world.
                                            —Frederick Saunders
The use of money is all the advantage there is in having
money.   —Benjamin Franklin
The deepest depth of vulgarism is that of setting up
money as the ark of the covenant.   —Carlyle
Make all you can, save all you can, give all you can.
                                                      —Wesley
Money is not required to buy one necessity of the soul.
                                                      —Thoreau
Without a rich heart wealth is an ugly beggar.
                                                      —Emerson
If we command our wealth, we shall be rich and free; if
our wealth commands us, we are poor indeed. We are
bought by the enemy with the treasure in our own coffers.
                                                      —Burke
There is a burden of care in getting riches, fear in deep-
ening them, temptation in using them, guilt in abusing
them, sorrow in losing them, and a burden of account at
  last to be given up concerning them.—Matthew Henry
It is not money, but the love of money, which is the root
of all evil.   —Hilliard
                                            — *Hight C. Moore*

Ill fares the land to hastening ills a prey,
Where wealth accumulates and men
decay.
                                            — *Oliver Goldsmith*

In 1923, eight of the world's most successful financiers met in Chicago. They were men who had found the secret of making money.

In Milwaukee, that same year, a champion was crowned at the 23rd Annual ABC Tournament, the world's most important bowling tournament.

AMF star bowler, Evelyn Teal, who was born in 1923, did some research and found out where these men are, forty years later.

1. The president of the largest independent steel company, Charles Schwab, died bankrupt, living on borrowed money for five years before his death.
2. The president of the largest gas company, Howard Hopson, became insane.
3. The greatest wheat speculator, Arthur Cotton, died abroad insolvent.
4. The president of the New York Stock Exchange, Richard Whitney, was sentenced to Sing Sing Penitentiary.
5. A member of the President's Cabinet, Albert Fall, was pardoned from prison so he could die at home.
6. The greatest "bear" on Wall Street, Jesse Livermore, committed suicide.
7. The head of the world's greatest monopoly, Ivar Kreuger, committed suicide.
8. The president of the Bank of International Settlements, Leon Frazier, committed suicide.

— *Evelyn Teal*

A Different Drummer

Why should we be in such a desperate haste to succeed and in such desperate enterprises? If a man does not keep pace with his companions, perhaps it is because he hears a different drummer.

However mean your life is, meet it and live it; do not shun it and call it hard names. It is not so bad as you are.

It looks poorest when you are richest. The fault-finder will find faults even in paradise. Love your life, poor as it is. You may perhaps have some pleasant, thrilling, glorious hours, even in a poorhouse. The setting sun is reflected from the windows of the almshouse as brightly as from the rich man's abode; the snow melts before its door as early in the spring.

Do not trouble yourself much to get new things, whether clothes or friends. Sell your clothes and keep your thoughts. God will see that you do not want society. If I were confined to a garret all my days, like a spider, the world would be just as large to me while I had my thoughts about me.

It is life near the bone where it is sweetest. You are defended from being a trifler. No man loses ever on a lower level by magnanimity on a higher. Superfluous wealth can buy superfluities only. Money is not required to buy one necessity of the soul.

— Henry David Thoreau

Concern for the poor has made phenomenal progress since the beginning of the twentieth century. Frank Laubach, renowned world missionary, lists in his book, The World is Learning Compassion, the following facts: In 1900 the women in Boston were getting $5 a week; the average earnings of laboring men was $500 a year. . . Andrew Carnegie's income was more than $10 million a year. The income of his workers was $460 a year! An unskilled laborer got $1.50 a day. In England it was far worse. Among the mine workers, wages, hours, and sanitation were "a stench in the nostrils of decency." The treatment of children was even worse. Dr. Laubach says that Henry Ford was the first to change the old oppressive conditions when he raised wages to $5.00 a day.

About this time John D. Rockefeller and others established great foundations for the promotion of the welfare of the poor of the world. It should be added here that Rockefeller lost his health at 55 and was given up by doctors to die of ulcers and other ailments. The story goes that "a little country preacher" lovingly informed him that he would recover if he would give his life to God and quit thinking totally of making more money. Rockefeller accepted the challenge. He began giving a portion of his money to good causes, finally establishing the Rockefeller Foundation which is operating to bless people to this day. A chapter could be written on his philanthropy.

Mr. Rockefeller regained his health and lived into his nineties. His philosophy, which he passed on to his children and grandchildren was:

1. make all the money you can earn
2. give away 10%
3. save 10%
4. spend the remainder

Dr. Laubach says that a little later seven thousand foundations were formed with total assets of seven billion dollars—among them were Ford, Rockefeller, Carnegie, Duke, Sloan, Kellog, and others.

No, there is no reason to believe that the human race has lost its compassion.

— *R.B. Phillips*

Suffer Little Children

A Roman father could legally put his child to the sword—an iron custom truly, but almost merciful when compared with the barbed abuses inflicted upon quivering child-flesh in later centuries of the Christian era. Medieval ignorance dispatched thousands on a Children's Crusade to perish of hunger and cold on the way or to be butchered and enslaved by Moslems. But probably no agonies ever inflicted upon tiny creatures can parallel the brutal exploitation of children during the Industrial Revolution.

So enlightened a man as Alexander Hamilton considered it a great boon that the new cloth-making machinery did not require the strength of able-bodied men, but could be operated by girls and boys. In the first factory in the United States, founded in 1790, all the operators were between the ages of seven and twelve; their employer rejoiced that their occupation relieved them of the "dangers of falling into vice and guilt." In Lowell, Massachusetts, after the Civil War, tots of ten worked 14 hours a day, beginning at 4:15 A.M. and working till 7:45 P.M. After this crushing stint, they were expected to perform household tasks and attend evening classes. If a fatigue-blinded child lost an arm or leg, or if a little girl's scalp were torn off by an unshielded belt catching her pigtails, it was just a minor tragedy and no compensation was offered or expected. To bag these diminutive slaves, agents from the mills canvassed the homes of the poor, hiring any child "old enough to stand on its legs." The father usually exercised his legal right to collect the wages of his children, which sometimes amounted to $2 for a 70-hour week!

American employers justified these abuses in terms of morality (i.e., it was sinful for a child to "eat the bread of idleness"), but in England mill owners asserted that child labor must not be restricted because children would starve to death unless gainful work were provided. Hence when a baby of four entered the coal mines plenty of "gainful work" was laid on his pitiful shoulders! He was harnessed dog-fashioned to a small truck and forced to drag coal on his hands and knees through passages too small to admit the body of a man. In the Birmingham blast furnaces boy apprentices stoked fires from 6 A.M. until 11 P.M., then for relaxation staggered into a nearby gin shop.

Until 1875 there was no tribunal in the world to which

a child could appeal for mercy. A parent or master might flog or starve a child with impunity; swine had more rights before the law. Indeed the law that first protected children against wanton cruelty was originally written for a dog!

In the winter of 1875 a voluntary missionary, Mrs. Etta Wheeler, found a woman dying of tuberculosis in a rickety tenement in New York City. Mrs. Wheeler asked the woman if there was anything she could do for her. The choked reply was: "My time is short, but I will die a peaceful death if you save that unhappy child next door." At that moment the sound of heavy blows and the screams of an agonized child were heard through the flimsy wall. When Mrs. Wheeler knocked at the door it was open by a hulking man who showered her with filthy language and threatened to throw her downstairs. In the corner was a girl about six years old, covered with rags, her face and arms streaked with blood.

Mrs. Wheeler reported the case to the nearest policeman who told her that he could not interfere with a father who felt inclined to beat his child. She next applied to a magistrate, but was informed that no legal power existed by which a parent could be prevented from "correcting" his child.

Finally Mrs. Wheeler laid the case before Elbridge Gerry, counsel for the Society for the Prevention of Cruelty to Animals. Mr. Gerry decided that the child might be rescued as a "little animal." Officers of the Society forcibly entered the tenement, seized the whip and scissors with which the girl's face and body had been gashed, and brought her case before the Supreme Court of New York. Here it was adjudged that the man and woman who had beaten and cut Mary Ellen with scissors (they were foster parents who had adopted her from an orphanage) were guilty of criminal conduct, and they were sentenced to a year in prison.

— *Henry Morton Robinson*

Lord God, I have walked from agency to agency asking for work, and been refused.

I have seen men, women, and children standing in long lines in front of a stone building awaiting their daily rations.

I have rested in the public square and seen the seeds of agitation sown in the fertile soil of discouraged minds.

I have welcomed the temporary respite of relief work, taking dictation from a college-bred man, himself a relief worker, who wrote of 'vocational maladjustments' and 'minor tragedy of blind-alley jobs.'

I have waited upon death in a general hospital where children's very bones were dissolving because of malnutrition.

I have known young boys with freckles standing out grotesquely against white faces and eyes glassy from hunger asking for "housework."

I have seen college girls, one a Phi Beta Kappa, who, unable to get positions in their chosen vocations, applied for Christmas work in a 5-10-15 cent store—and had even that refused them.

I have watched hope, ambition, dreams die out of faces, to be replaced by resignation in the old, and by doubt and desperation in the young.

And I have felt a nameless terror creep into mine.

Lord God,

Have I, and a million others like me, a destiny?

And if so, is it worth attaining?

— *Margaret Cosgrove*

———•◆◆◆•———

O God—when I have food,
Help me to remember the hungry;
When I have work, Help me to remember the jobless;
When I have a warm home, Help me to remember those
   who have no home at all;

When I am without pain, Help me to remember those
   who suffer— and remembering, Help me to destroy my complacency, and bestir my compassion—
   and be concerned enough to help,
By word and deed, those who cry out for what we take
   for granted.
Amen.   — *Samuel F. Pugh*

Forgive Me, Child

Forgive me child,
For harshly scolding you
Altho we both must tacitly admit your dullness.
Keep your eyes off me; they accuse me.
Your mother at fifteen married your father.
She went to the third grade in six years of school.
Your father went to the fifth grade in nine years of
   school.
You have six brothers and one sister.
You eat boiled potatoes moistened with salt pork fat
Twice a day, and warmed-up potatoes in the morning.
You wear what is given you.
You have no toothbrush.
You have no space in which to take a bath.
Your family spreads itself in a two-room shack.
Your only spot of brightness is my schoolroom.
O God, Help me make it bright!
                                  — *Natalie Nason*

If you had everything, where would you put it?
                           — *Author unknown*

Give me your tired, your poor,
Your huddled masses yearning to breathe free,
The wretched refuse of your teeming shores,
Send these, the homeless, the tempest-tossed to me;
I lift my lamp beside the golden door!
       — *Emma Lazarus, (Statue of Liberty Inscription)*

Hidden Curriculum

Gurney Chambers is dean of the school of education and psychology at Western Carolina University. He tells teachers about his school days on Hunting Creek in a remote section of Wilkes County in the hopes it will sensitize them to the pain of the "hidden curriculum":

"I came from a background of poverty. Most teachers come from the working class, and they can identify with this story very well.

"When I was in school, if you were anybody, you ate in the lunchroom. If you were a country hick, you took your lunch. Children, at a very early age, even in first grade, are painfully aware of these forces that are at work in the school. The effect of which is to impress upon them they are not as good as other students.

"In my own case, I divided the world into two groups, the rich and the poor. There was no in between. The rich kids were those who rested on blankets during the rest period and the poor kids were those who had to rest on newspapers. Many of us, I included, did not even have newspapers to bring to school because we didn't take the paper. So Miss Barber would save her newspapers. She was a marvelous human being, still living, 93 years old. She would take newspapers out of the closet and spread them on the oily wooden floors they had in those days. I can remember thinking at that time I would love to rest on a blanket.

"I recall most vividly this lunchroom—taking your lunch split in the sixth grade. We, as very young children, naive and unsophisticated, nevertheless made this very fine distinction among the students by what they brought their lunch in. There was also a hierarchy of the contents of those containers, even a hierarchy of what those were wrapped in.

"If you really were nobody and felt you just couldn't cope and went into school swinging a lard bucket, this was at the bottom of the hierarchy.

"Of course, families in my circle would cook with lard and once the lard had been used, the pail made a nice lunch pail. But we were ashamed of it. On the same level was the Karo syrup pail.

"Better than the bucket, but not much better, was the bag in which something had been bought, for example a light bread bag, a sugar bag, or a coffee bag.. . .

"The truth for any individual is the way he perceives it. If we thought the teachers or our peers were looking with disfavor, it was a painful thing. In my family there were six stair-step children and my father died when he was 29. My mother would pack the same thing for each child and if you didn't like what it was—well, that was tough.

"Above the bag in which something had been purchased was a wrinkled and greasy brown poke, not as good as a brand-new, crisp sack. Grease was a dead giveaway. It told your peers it had been used before. I can still recall with some pain that my mother insisted we bring our bags home and I was ashamed to let anyone see me folding that bag and putting it in my pocket.

"Next best was the clean bag. Tops was the store-bought lunch pail with the college pennants on it.

"At the bottom of the contents hierarchy were cornbread and a green onion or a sweet potato. Anything that smacked of the country was inferior. A little bit better, but not much, was a biscuit of fatback with the skin still on it. A biscuit of blackberry jam was better still. Better than a biscuit with meat or jam was one with peanut butter because it was bought. A biscuit of country ham even, believe it or not, was something to be ashamed of. I would have traded a biscuit of country ham for a sandwich of light bread and mayonnaise. Anything made with light bread was superior to anything made with a biscuit.

"I had a friend whose father was an insurance salesman and his mother a teacher. He had a middle-class family, but occasionally brought his lunch in a store-bought lunch pail. I can recall sitting, eating my biscuits and looking over at his pimiento cheese sandwich and thinking it was so luxurious looking. His mother had cut it into two triangles and peeled the crust from the bread and that represented the ultimate.

"The way Miss Star, a very sensitive teacher, handled this—realizing we were bothered by these kinds of things—was that one day she announced she had noticed that some of the children brought to school these wonderful biscuits of jam and meat and that she just loved biscuits, but couldn't make them. She wondered if we would be willing to trade our biscuits for some of her sandwiches.

"Today a country ham biscuit is my idea of a really great lunch. There never will be anything better than biscuits and milk gravy and 'western meat,' fatback with the skin still on it. We don't have to eat that now at home. We have it for nostalgic reasons. What I love most today is what I was ashamed of then."

— Nancy Brower

———•◆◆•■—

Man's attitude toward money matters has been described in these words:

If a man runs after money, he's money mad; if he keeps it, he's a miser; if he spends it, he's a playboy; if he doesn't get it, he's a ne'er-do-well; if he gets it without working, he's a parasite; if he doesn't try to get it, he lacks ambition; and if he accumulates it after a lifetime of hard work, he's a fool who never got anything out of life.

— Author unknown

———•◆◆•■—

The strong get stronger until they collapse; the weak get weaker until they rebel; then they change places and repeat the process—The strong and powerful never give up power until they have to.

— Sidney Harris

Man with the Hoe, J.F. Millet.

    Bowed by the weight of centuries he leans
    Upon his hoe land gazes on the ground. . .
              — *Edwin Markham*

We need not fear alienation from God.

I feel Him when I feed a beggar. I serve Him when I serve my neighbor. I love Him when I love my friend. I praise Him when I praise the wise and good of any race or time. I shun Him when I shun the leper. I forgive Him when I forgive my enemies. I wound Him when I wound a human being. I forget Him when I forget my duty to others. If I am cruel or unjust or resentful or envious or inhospitable toward any man or woman or child, I am guilty of all these things toward God. Inasmuch as ye have done it unto the least of these my Brethren, ye have done it unto me.

              — *John Burroughs*

I suspect more people are confused about the subject of money than any other matter except possibly sex.

It is a truism that "money can't bring happiness," but most people are willing to take their chances. This is because the truism is only a half-truth—and this is where the confusion sets in.

What money can buy is more negative than positive. It can buy relief or release from certain kinds of unhappiness. It can smooth out kinks, unravel complications, and diminish worries in specific areas.

The power of money is broad, but shallow. It has not made any family happier, or any marriage better founded—but it may help compensate for a miserable family life or an incompatible marriage.

It is a palliative, a bandage, and sometimes a prophylactic; but it cannot heal a psychic wound, or prevent one, or in any way conduce to happiness in an affirmative sense.

And while there can be no such thing as too much good health, there is such a thing as too much money. We have all seen what it does to marriages, to families, to business and social relationships. Not to mention the individuals who cannot possess it without being possessed by it.

To suppose that money is of little consequence in the overall scheme of things is to be a fool. But, equally, to suppose that our lives would be all strawberries-and-cream if only our income were doubled, or trebled, is to live in a fool's paradise. All you have to do is read the annals of the very rich to be disabused of this simple notion.

Money removes certain kinds of problems from life—but then other problems inevitably move in to replace them; and sometimes these new problems are more intractable than the ones they displaced.

There is another deep psychological trap about money that is rarely recognized. As long as we are short of money, we can scramble to get more, in the hope that when we reach the pinnacle, our personal happiness will then be achievable.

But if we have all the money we need, and more, and our personal lives are still unsatisfactory, we can non longer blame it on lack of funds, and are forced to look inside ourselves for the reason. It is then that the worm begins to eat at our innards, and we realize that no amount of money is going to make much difference.

The pursuit of money prevents us from confronting ourselves in our existential nakedness, often for a lifetime. Take away this pursuit, and we are forced to ask ourselves what we are, rather than what we have.

Little wonder that most of us would rather scramble than scrutinize.

— *Sydney Harris*

Values

In our town, the old man living
In the mansion on the hill, died—
Which is of course the common fate of all—
Rich and poor alike.
School was closed for the day;
Business came to a standstill.
"O why," I said, "should this
Occur in our town?"
Men have died from time to time—
Are in their graves, and worms have eaten their flesh—
Few by choice.
Sun and moon have not changed their courses.
So why this man?
I asked James, he's in the seventh grade,
And usually knows everything.
"He owns most of the town, doesn't he?" he said.
"That's about as powerful as
Anyone gets around here."

My great uncle was a kind and gentle Methodist
preacher,
A circuit rider, they said.
He claimed no money nor fame;
Everybody loved him but none feared him.
When he retired at seventy,
He received an official letter
From a group of his parishioners saying,
"Would you come and settle here with us?
We believe we would have a better community
With you among us."
Which man's life was most rewarding?

— *R.B. Phillips*

Fighting Stallions, Anne Hyatt Huntington. Courtesy of Brookgreen Gardens.

> Build me straight, O worthy master,
> Staunch and strong, a goodly vessel,
> That will laugh at all disaster,
> And with wave and whirlwind wrestle.
>   — *Henry Wadsworth Longfellow*

COURAGE

Courage consists of doing the thing you ought to do whether you want to or not.

Many things are hard to do; it takes a little more time and effort to do the impossible.

Once when a ship was sinking off Cape Hatteras, a cost guardsman was warned he could never get out to the ship and return. He replied without hesitation, "I have to go; I don't have to come back."

"I am determined never to stop until I have come to the end and achieved my purpose."
—The motto of David Livingstone

The Country's Call

Give me men to match my mountains;
　　Men, to match my inland plains;
Men with empires in their purpose;
　　Men with eras in their brains.

Give me men to match my prairies:
　　Men, to match my inland seas—
Men whose thoughts shall pave a pathway
　　Up to ampler destinies.
— Author unknown

I do not choose to be a common man. It is my right to be uncommon—if I can. I seek opportunity, not security. I do not wish to be a kept citizen, humbled and dulled by having the state look after me. I want to take the calculated risk; to dream and to build; to fail and to succeed. I refuse to barter the incentive for a dole. I prefer the challenge of life to the guaranteed existence; the thrill of fulfillment to the stale claim of Utopia. I will not trade a freedom for a beneficence nor my dignity for a handout. I will never cower before any master nor bend to any threat. It is my heritage to stand erect, proud, and unafraid; to think and act for myself, enjoy the benefit of my creations, and to face the world boldly and say, "This I have done. . . "

— *Creed of Abilities, Inc.,*
(a group of disabled men and women)

———•◆◆•——

Discouraged? Think Of Lincoln

When Abraham Lincoln was a young man he ran for the legislature in Illinois and was badly swamped. He next entered a business, failed, and spent 17 years of his life paying up the debts of a worthless partner. He fell in love with a beautiful young woman to whom he became engaged; then she died. Entering politics, he ran for Congress and was badly defeated. He then tried to get an appointment to the United States Land Office, but failed. He became a candidate for the United States Senate and was badly defeated. In 1856 he became a candidate for the vice presidency and was again defeated. In 1858 he was defeated by Douglas. But in the face of all this defeat and failure, he eventually achieved the highest success attainable in life, and undying fame to the end of time.

— *Author unknown*

From the moment of independence on the Fourth of July, 1776, the 56 men who voted for adoption of the document became marked men. They were hounded by the British, some were captured and held prisoner, others saw their property destroyed, two lost sons in the Revolution, another had two sons captured, and nine of the 56 either died from wounds received in the fighting or the hardship of the war.

Not all were victims of privation, of course. Thomas Jefferson and John Adams became Presidents of the United States and many others rose to high positions in the national and state government.

— Author unknown

———•◆•◆•■—

Back in 1892 Dr. Walter Rauschenbusch, the powerful prophet of Christian social justice, wrote an article entitled "Pilate's Washbowl." According to the story, on the evening of that day when Pilate washed his hands of responsibility for the fate of Christ, the washbowl disappeared from the palace. It is not known who took it. But ever since that time the washbowl has been abroad in the world, carried by infernal hands wherever it is needed, and men are constantly joining the group who perform their ablutions therein. Whenever a statesman suppresses principles because he might jeopardize the success of his party; whenever good citizens refuse to participate in public affairs on the pretext that such involves politics; whenever an editor remains silent when a righteous cause is at stake for fear an expression of his views will injure circulation; whenever a preacher sees Dives exploiting Lazarus and does not protest because Dives contributes to his salary; whenever Christians ignore their responsibilities for social justice and moral welfare in their communities— all of these are using Pilate's Washbowl, the water of which is poured by the devil himself.

— R.B. Phillips

The Sprinter, R. Tait MacKensie. Photographer unknown.
Courtesy of Brookgreen Gardens.

My God, My God, keep me from turning back.
— *Author unknown*

He does not want them to be innocent only;
Pure because there is not a cloud;
Calm because there is no wind;
Honest because there is no temptation;
Loyal because there is no danger.
We cannot know Thy stillness until it is broken.
There is no music in the silence
Until we have heard the roar of battle!
We cannot see Thy beauty until it is shaded.
— *Author unknown*

When the Roman soldiers sought to arrest Jesus in
the Garden he replied "I am He." Then they all fell
backward on the ground.
— *John 18:6*

When Charles Lindbergh landed his small plane in Paris in 1927 and was offered wine, he replied: "Please give me a glass of milk and a bath."

A man who wants to lead the orchestra must turn his back on the crowd.

— *Author unknown*

They say the little efforts I make will do no good;
They never will prevail to tip the hovering scales
When justice hangs in balance.
I don't think I ever thought they would;
But I am prejudiced beyond debate
In favor of my right
To choose which side shall feel
The stubborn ounces of my weight.

— *Brando Overstreet*

An ancient Greek legend tells how a barbarian chieftain sought to honor Alexander the Great by giving him three noble dogs of matchless courage. Soon afterward, Alexander decided to test the dogs. He had a stag brought before him; but the dogs only yawned and went to sleep. Then he had a deer and an antelope put into the park with them; but the dogs seemed scarcely aware of their presence. Disgusted, the king ordered the dogs to be killed.

Some time later the chieftain returned to ask about his dogs. When he was told what had been done to them he cried, "O Alexander, you are a great king, but you are a foolish man. You showed them a stag and a deer and an antelope, and they paid no attention, but if you had turned a lion and a tiger loose on them you would have seen what brave dogs I had given you."

— *Author unknown*

The Winds Of Fate

One ship drives east, another west,
   By the selfsame winds that blow.
'Tis the set of the sail, and not the gale,
   That determines the way they go.
Like the winds of the sea are the ways of Fate
   As we voyage along thru life.
'Tis the set of a sail that decides its goal,
   And not the calm or the strife.

                     — *Ella Wheeler Wilcox*

How dull it is to pause, to make an end,
To rust unburnished, not to shine in use!
As though to breath were life! Life piled on life
Were all too little, and of one to me
Little remains; but every hour is saved
From that eternal silence, something more
A bringer of new things: and vile it were
For some three suns to store and hoard myself
And this gay spirit yearning in desire
To follow knowledge like a sinking star,
Beyond the utmost bound of human thought.
           . . .
There lies the port; the vessel puffs her sail;
There gloom the dark, broad seas. My mariners,
Souls that have toiled, and wrought, and thought with
    me
That ever with a frolic welcome took
The thunder and the sunshine, and opposed
Free hearts, free foreheads—you and I are old;
Old age hath yet his honor and his toil.
Death closes all. But something ere the end,
Some work of noble note may yet be done,
Not unbecoming men that strove with gods.
The lights begin to twinkle from the rocks;
The long day wanes; the slow moon climbs; the deep
Moans round with many voices.

Come, my friends,
'Tis not too late to seek a newer world.
Push off, and sitting well in order smite
The sounding furrows; for my purpose holds
To sail beyond the sunset, and the baths
Of all the western stars, until I die.
. . .
It may be that the gulfs will wash us down;
It may be we shall touch the Happy Isles,
And see the great Achilles, whom we knew.
Though much is taken, much abides; and though
We are now that strength which in old days
Moved earth and heaven, that which we are, we are—
One equal temper of heroic hearts,
Made weak by time and fate, but strong in will
To strive, to seek, to find, and not to yield.

— *Alfred Lord Tennyson, (Ulysses)*

Paul Bunyan, Robert Pippenger. Courtesy of Brookgreen Gardens.

Keep me from turning back; my hand is on the plow, my faltering hand; But all in front of me is untilled land. . .

— *Author unknown*

Hunting An Easy Berth?

Henry Ward Beecher once received a letter from a student asking him for an easy berth. To this he replied, "Young man, you cannot be an editor; do not try the law; do not think of the ministry; let alone all ships and merchandise; abhor politics; don't practice medicine; be not a farmer, a soldier, or a sailor; don't study; don't think. None of these are easy. Oh, my son, you have come into a hard world. I know of only one easy place in it and that is in the grave.!"

— *Christian Union Herald*

———

Submit to pressure from peers and you move down to their level. Speak up for your own beliefs and you invite them up to your level. If you move with the crowd, you'll get no further than the crowd. When 40 million people believe in a dumb idea, it's still a dumb idea. Simply swimming with the tide leaves you nowhere.

So if you believe in something that's good, honest, and bright, stand up for it. Maybe your peers will get smart and drift your way.

— *Harry J. Gray, chairman of United Technology*

———

Keep me from turning back; my hand is on the plow,
my faltering hand, But all in front of me is untilled land,
The wilderness and solitary place, The lonely desert
with its interspace.... My courage is outworn. Keep me
from turning back.
The handles of my plow with tears are wet,
The shares with rust are spoiled, and yet, and yet,
My God, My God, Keep me from turning back!

— *Author unknown*

If a man has not found something he will die for he's not fit to live.

— *Martin Luther King, Jr.*

———◆◆◆——

I am only one; but I am one. I cannot do everything, but I can do something. That which I can do, I must do; and by the grace of God, I will do.

— *Edward E. Hale*

———◆◆◆——

Death, Photo Pat Mullinnix.

Those who love the living feel life to be all the sweeter and dearer because it is so transitory.
— *from Philosophy of the Christian Religion*

SUFFERING and DEATH

However we are loath to admit it the knowledge of suffering and death is necessary for life to be meaningful.

It brings new meaning into life, defines it, and makes it great. Time takes on new value, and love and affections become nobler.

Unselfishness and sacrifice for others surface, when we know that time here is limited. Devotion to loved ones takes on new life when we are aware that we shall some time be separated. The limited time drives our thoughts toward eternity, and thus bids us live in earnest.

The Child's Grave

As through the land as ere we went, and plucked the
    ripened ears,
We fell out, my wife and I, O we fell out, I know not why,
And kissed again with tears. And blessings on the falling
    out
That all the more endears, When we fall out with those
    we love
And kiss again with tears! For when we came where lies
    the child
We lost in other years, There above the little grave,
O, there above the little grave, We kissed again with tears.
— *Alfred Lord Tennyson*

Death

Harold Kushner tells us in *All You've Wanted Isn't Enough:* ". . . God does not redeem us from death. We will all die one day. But He redeems us from the shadow of death, from letting our lives be paralyzed by the fear of death."

The philosopher, Horace Kallen, marked his seventy-third birthday by writing: "There are persons who shape their lives by the fear of death, and persons who shape their lives by the joy and satisfaction of life. The former live dying; the latter die living.

"I have no fear of death because I feel that I have lived. I have loved and I have been loved. . . . I can look forward to the last act of my life, however long or short it may be, in the knowledge that I have finally figured out who I am and how to handle life.

"I walk unafraid through the valley and shadow, not only because God is with me now but because He has guided me to this point. There is no way to prevent dying. But the cure for the fear of death is to make sure you have lived."

— R.B. Phillips

Death

O Death, thou art a cruel and wanton master!
Whence comest thou, unwelcomed guest?
Keep thy highway—onward—faster!
Go thy way and let us rest!

Myriads you have borne away,
Who seemed on earth to be so blessed.
Upon each fevered brow you lay
Your icy hand in night or day.

— R.B. Phillips

Inscription on the tomb of Robert L. Stevenson, written for himself shortly before his death in Samoa:
"Here he lies where he longed to be;
Home is the sailor, home from the sea,
And the hunter home from the hills."

———

Break, break, break,
On thy cold gray stones, O Sea!
And I would that my tongue could uttter
The thoughts that arise in me.

O, well for the fisherman's boy,
That he shouts with his sister at play!
O, well for the sailor lad,
That he sings in his boat on the bay!

And the stately ships go on
To their haven under the hill;
But O for the touch of a vanished hand,
And the sound of a voice that is still!

Break, break, break,
At the foot of thy crags, O Sea!
But the tender grace of a day that is dead
Will never come back to me.
— *Alfred Lord Tennyson*

———

And God said, "Go down, Death, go down, Go down to Savannah, Georgia, Down in Yamacrow, and find Sister Caroline! She's borne the burden and heat of the day, She's labored long in my vineyard, And she's tired—she's weary—Go down Death, and bring her to me."
— *James Wildon Johnson*

The changes wrought by death are in themselves so sharp and final, and so terrible and melancholy in their consequences that the thing stands alone in man's experience, and has no parallel upon earth. It outdoes all other accidents because it is the last of them. Sometimes it leaps suddenly upon its victims, like a Thug; sometimes it lays a regular siege and creeps upon their citadel during a score of years. And when the business is done, there is sore havoc made in other people's lives, and a pin knocked out by which many subsidiary friendships hung together. There are empty chairs, solitary walks, and single beds at night. Again in taking away our friends, death does not take them away utterly but leaves behind a mocking, tragical, and soon intolerable residue, which must be hurriedly concealed. Hence a whole chapter of sights and customs striking to the mind, from the pyramids of Egypt to the gibbets and dule trees of medieval Europe. The poorest persons have a bit of pageant going toward the tomb.

— *Robert Louis Stevenson*

Music I Heard

Music I heard with you was more than music,
And bread I broke with you was more than bread;
Now that I am without you, all is desolate;
All that was once so beautiful is dead.

Your hands once touched this table and this silver,
And I have seen your fingers hold this glass.
These things do not remember you, beloved—
And yet your touch upon them will not pass.

For it was in my heart you moved among them,
And blessed them with your hands and with your eyes;
And in my heart they will remember always—
They knew you once, O beautiful and wise.

— *Conrad Aiken*

Dig a hole in your garden of thoughts.

Into it put all your disillusions, disappointments, regrets, worries, troubles, doubts, and fears, and—forget.

Cover well with the earth of fruitfulness, water it from the well of content.

Sow on top again the seeds of hope, courage, strength, patience, and love.

Then, when the time of gathering comes, may your harvest be a rich and plentiful one.

— *Author unknown*

Daughter of Pyrrha, Lorado Taft. Courtesy of Brookgreen Gardens.

Pain strips the mask from every soul,
And leaves it naked pure and whole.
— *Mae Winkler Goodman*

Share sorrow and it divides in half; share joy and it is doubled.

— *Author unknown*

———————

. . . So live, that when thy summons comes to join
The innumerable caravan, which moves
To that mysterious realm, where each shall take
His chamber in the silent halls of death,
Thou go not, like the quarry-slave at night,
Scourged to his dungeon, but, sustained and soothed
By an unfaltering trust, approach thy grave,
Like one who wraps the drapery of his couch
About him, and lies down to pleasant dreams.

— *William Cullen Bryant*

———————

I walked a mile with pleasure, and she chattered all the
    way
But ne'er a thing I learned from her, as we walked along
    the way.
I walked a mile with sorrow, and ne'er a word said she.
But oh, the things I learned from her as we walked along
    the way.

— *Robert Browning Hamilton*

———————

Be still, sad heart, and cease repining;
Behind the clouds is the sun still shining;
Thy fate is the common fate of all,
Into each life some rain must fall,
Some days must be dark and dreary.

— *Henry Wadsworth Longfellow*

How To Live With Illness

1. Talk about the illness. If it's cancer, call it cancer. You can't make life normal again by trying to hide what is wrong.
2. Accept death as a part of life. It is.
3. Consider each day as another day of life, a gift from God to be enjoyed as fully as possible.
4. Realize that life is never going to be perfect. It wasn't before, and it won't be now.
5. Pray. It isn't a sign of weakness, it's sign of strength.
6. Learn to live with your illness instead of considering yourself dying from it. We are all dying in some manner.
7. Put your friends and relatives at ease. If you don't want pity, don't ask for it.
8. Make all practical arrangements for funerals, wills, etc., and make certain your family understands them.
9. Set new goals, realize your limitations. Sometimes the things of life become the most enjoyable.
10. Discuss your problems with your family. Include the children if possible. After all, your problem is not an individual one. Have a good day. . . make it count.

— Orville Kelly

———◆◆◆———

Healing from Grievous Trials

There are positive uses of grief. One is that it gives us the opportunity to deal with unresolved conflict in the relationship which has been severed by separation. Perhaps we felt some estrangement between ourselves and the one we have lost. Maybe there were unanswered questions, unmade decisions, unsettled differences. Grief is our chance to deal with these negative feelings. Grief provides occasions for expressing our sorrow, and for putting our thoughts about the lost loved one in perspective.

Grief can also help us to stop denying our losses. By grieving we come to the point of letting go, of permitting our lost loved ones to take the appropriate place in our lives, and that is among those from whom we are separated by the mystery of death.

Further, I believe that grief can be a great teacher. We would not choose its instruction if we had a choice, but we can use it. We can learn about the fragility of human existence, that what we love most dearly we hold by the slenderest of threads, that the resources within us are greater than we imagined before we needed them, that God's grace really is sufficient, and that day by day in unpredictable ways he provides what we have to have to make it.

. . . Grief may be not only a great teacher, but also an enormously useful power in our effort to understand and aid others who grieve.

If you have known grief, you ought to be able to help somebody else get through it. God knows, there is enough to go around. If we will only take time to look and help.

— *L.D. Johnson, Furman University Chaplain*

———◆◆◆———

While we many not like to accept it, adversity and suffering are often the hammer and anvil used to beat out the stuff of which great men and women are made. Herman Endler, who at the age of forty suffered a stroke that left him totally disabled, wrote:

Cripple him, and you have a Sir Walter Scott.

Lock him in a prison cell, and you have a John Bunyan.

Bury him in the snows of Valley Forge, and you have a George Washington.

Raise him in abject poverty, and you have an Abraham Lincoln.

Subject him to religious persecution, and you have a Disraeli.

Spit on him, humiliate him, crucify him, then he forgives you, and you have a Jesus Christ.

Strike him down with infantile paralysis, and he become Franklin D. Roosevelt.

Deafen a genius composer who continues to write some of the world's most beautiful music, and you have a Beethoven.

Have him born black in a society filled with racial discrimination, and you have a Booker T. Washington, Marion Anderson, George Washington Carver, and Martin Luther King.

Make him the first child to survive in a poor Italian family of eighteen children, and you have an Enrico Caruso.

Amputate an arm and leg of an aspiring actor, and you have a James Stacy.

Call a slow learner "retarded" and write him off as uneducated, and you have an Albert Einstein.

Afflict him with asthma as a child, and you have a Theodore Roosevelt.

Stab him with rheumatic pains until he cannot sleep without an opiate, and you have a Steinmetz.

Put him in a grease pit in a locomotive roundhouse, and you have a Walter P. Chrysler.

Make him second fiddle in an obscure South African orchestra, and you have a Toscanini.

— *Herman Endler*

———•·•◆•◆•·•———

A hero is not fed on sweets,
Daily his iron heart he eats:
Chambers of the great are jails,
And head winds right for royal sails.
— *Ralph Waldo Emerson*

Pain rips the mask from every soul
And leaves it naked, pure and whole.
No subterfuge can still remain
Beneath the ruthless claws of pain;
Beneath its keen incisive knife
One comes face to face with life,
Raw, elemental, clean as bone,
When each must meet himself, alone.
Stripped of beauty, sham, and pelf. . .
Pain acquaints man with himself!
— *Mae Winkler Goodman*

Tribulation is the way to triumph. The valley way opens into the highway. Tribulation's imprint is on all great things. Crowns are cast in crucibles. Chains of character that wind about the feet of God are forged in earthly flames. No man is greatest victor till he has trodden the winepress of woe. Jesus said, "In this world ye shall have

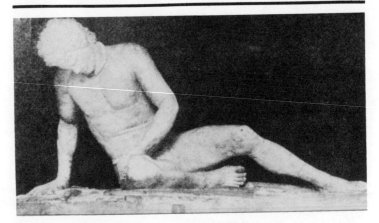

The Dying Gladiator, Art Institute of Chicago.

Cowards die many times before their deaths;
The valiant never taste of death but once.
— *William Shakespeare, (Julius Caesar)*

tribulation." He also said, "Be of good cheer, I have over-come the world."

Bloodstains mark the steps that lead to thrones, scars are the price of selfless ones. Our crowns will be wrested from the giants we conquer. Grief has always been the lot of greatness. It is an open secret. Tribulation has always marked the trail of the true reformer. It is the story of Paul, Luther, Savonarola, Knox, Wesley, and the rest of the mighty army. They came through great tribulation to their place of power.

Every good book has been written with the author's blood. There are they who have come out of great tribulation. Who was the peerless poet of the Greeks? Homer. But that illustrious singer was blind; Milton wrote *Paradise Lost* while blind. John Bunyan wrote *Pilgrim's Progress* in Bedford jail. Most of the great epistles of Paul were written in jail.

— Author unknown

Pain Has A Message

Pain is a signal of danger. British author C.S. Lewis, in his book, *The Problem of Pain*, says that pain announces "something is wrong and needs diagnosis and healing." He goes on to say, "God whispers to us in our pleasure, speaks in our conscience, and shouts in our pain."

But for many people, pain—either physical or mental—goes far beyond being a warning signal. It can become a disease in itself. It can destroy the personality.

Some pain can be alleviated. Some of it cannot. But all pain is sending us a message.

Pain can be a signal to stop, to seek the cause. It can also be a signal to move, to seek that remedy. Suffering sweeps away the revival. Pain can remind us to use each moment in the best possible way because our moments are limited.

— Christophers

The Legend Of Jubal

In the old, soft sweet days before man knew death,
His descendants lived in gladsome idleness;
They played, they sang, they danced in life that had no
   gravity.
Then came death and all its darkness.
Man then learned there would come to his own race
A sleep from which there was no awakening.

A new meaning stole into life, defined it and made it
   great.
Time took on new value and affections became nobler.
Men thought of themselves and their deeds more truly
When they saw that night came when no man could
   work.
Friends and families lived in a more tender light.
When the sun was known to shine for only a season.

The limits set to time drove their thoughts toward
   eternity.
The idea that death would claim them bade them to live
   in earnest.
Men came to feel that there was something greater than
   play.
Death had breathed into life a new spirit,
Out of which all tragic and heroic things come.
Without it men would have no kinship with the infinite;
For the finite would have been enough for them.

The thought of possible loss touches with tenderness all
   relations of life.
It explains the watchfulness of the mother and the
   ungrudging labor of the father;
The solicitous care of the wife and affection and
   forethought of the husband.
Those who love the living feel life to be the sweeter and
   dearer,
Because it is so transitory.

He who writes these things once knew a man
Who was to him companion, friend and more than a
   brother.
We lived, we thought, we agreed, we argued together;
Together we walked on the hillsides and on the
   seashores.
We listened to the wind as it soughed through the trees.
And to the multitudinous laughter of the waves
As they broke upon the sandy beach.

Together we descended into the slums of a great city
Where no light was nor fragrance known;
We faced the worst depravity of our kind.
Each kept hope alive in the other,
And stimulated him to high endeavor and better
   purpose.
Of the two friends, one settled to be called home.
The other remained to work his tale of toil
Until his longer day be done.

But the one who died seemed to leave his spirit behind
In the breast of the man who survived; and has lived
   there ever since, and still lives;
Feeling as if the soul within him belonged to the man
   who died.
However man may conceive death it belongs to those
Sufferings by which mankind learns obedience, and is
   made perfect.
   — *Author unknown, adapted by R.B. Phillips from* The
            Philosophy of the Christian Religion

-----◄•♦♦•►-----

Trust Him when darkest thoughts assail thee.
Trust Him when thy faith is small.
Trust Him when to simply trust Him is the hardest thing
   of all.
   — *Christophers*

The Death Of Socrates

Then Crito made a sign to his slave, who was standing by, and the slave went out, and after some delay returned with the man who was to give the poison, carrying it prepared in a cup. When Socrates saw him, he asked, "You understand these things, my good sire, what I have to do?" "You have only to drink this," he replied, "and to walk about until your legs feel heavy, and then lie down, and it will act of itself." With that he handed the cup to Socrates who took it quite cheerfully. Socrates, without trembling and without any change of feature, looked up at the man with that fixed glance of his and asked, "What say you to making a libation from this draft? May I, or not?" "We only prepare so much as we think sufficient, Socrates," he answered. "I understand," said Socrates. "But I suppose that I may, and must, pray to the Gods that my journey hence may be prosperous: that is my prayer, be it so." With these words, he put the cup to his lips and drank the poison quite lively and cheerfully. Till then most of us had been able to control our grief fairly well; but when we saw him drinking and then the poison finished, we could do so no longer; my tears came first in spite of myself, and I covered my face and wept for myself; it was not for him, but at my own misfortune in losing such a friend . . . "What are you doing, my friends?" Socrates exclaimed . . . "I have heard that a man should die in silence. So calm yourselves and bear up."

When we heard that, we were ashamed, and we ceased from weeping. But we walked about until he said his legs were getting heavy, and then he lay down on his back, as he was told. And the man who gave the poison began to examine his feet and legs, from time to time. Then he pressed his foot hard and asked if there was any feeling in it; and Socrates said, "No:" and then his legs, and so higher and higher, and showed he was cold and stiff. And Socrates felt himself, and said that when it came to his heart, he should be gone. He was already growing cold above the groin, when he uncovered his face which had been covered, and spoke for the last time. "Crito," he said, "I owe a cock to Asclepius: Do not forget to pay it." "It shall be done," replied Crito. "Is there anything else that you wish?" He made no answer to this question; but after a short interval, there was movement, and the man uncovered him, and his eyes were fixed. Then Crito closed his mouth and eyes. Such was the end, Eshrecrates, of our friend, a man, I think, who was the wisest and justest, and the best man I have ever known.

— Plato, (Phaedo)

O death, where is thy sting?
O grave, where is thy victory?
— I Corinthians 15:55

How To Meet Sorrow

• Consider that the manner in which you receive your sorrow will affect, for good or bad, your entire subsequent life.

• Remind yourself that while death changes the circumstances of your association with your loved one, it does not separate you. Since "love can never lose its own" you will be conscious, in high moments, of your loved one's spiritual presence.

• Keep reminding yourself that your loved one is within the Father's house of many mansions and is surrounded by love and beauty.

• Look for opportunities to give comfort and healing to other people.

By helping to relieve their sorrow, your own will become easier to bear.

— Norman Vincent Peale

As a fond mother, when the day is o'er,
Leads by the hand her little child to bed,
Half willing, half reluctant to be led.
And leave his broken playthings on the floor,
Still gazing at them through the open door,
Nor wholly reassured and comforted
By promise of other in their stead,
Which, though more splendid, may not please him
    more;
So nature deals with us, and takes away
Our playthings one by one, and by the hand
Leads us to rest so gently, that we go
Scarce knowing if we wish to go or stay,
Being too full of sleep to understand
How far the unknown transcends what we know.

— *Henry Wadsworth Longfellow*

Nothing in life became him like the leaving it; he died
As one that had been studied in his death,
To throw away the dearest thing he owned
As 'twere a careless trifle.

— *William Shakespeare, (Macbeth)*

Stone walls do not a prison make nor iron bars a cage,
Minds innocent and quiet take that for a hermitage;
If I have freedom in my love and in my soul I'm free,
Angels alone, that soar above, enjoy such liberty.

– *Richard Lovelace*

Sorrows come to stretch out spaces in the heart for
joy.

— *Author unknown*

Suffering

If flowers reasoned, would they understand
Why suddenly the gardener's hand
   Uproots,
   Selects,
   Transplants
To give their roots more room, their leaves more air—
Would flowers misconstrue this care
   As wrath,
   Contempt,
   Disdain?
Or be content to let their beauty show
His wisdom. . . or demand to know
   His plan,
   Intent,
   Design?

— Jane W. Lauber

Who hath woe? who hath sorrow? who hath contentions? who hath babbling? who hath wounds without cause? who hath redness of eyes?

They that tarry long at the wine; they that go to seek mixed wine.

Look not thou upon the wine when it is red, when it giveth his colour in the cup, when it moveth itself aright.

At the last it biteth like a serpent, and stingeth like an adder.

Thine eyes shall behold strange women, and thine heart shall utter perverse things.

Yea, thou shalt be as he that lieth down in the midst of the sea, or as he that lieth upon the top of a mast.

They have stricken me, shall thou say, and I was not sick; they have beaten me, and I felt it not: when shall I awaken? I will seek it yet again.

— Proverbs 23:29–35

The Pain We Bring On Ourselves

We may not like to think so, but the roots of much suffering lie in our own desires. Modern science and psychology have confirmed what the major religious traditions have long taught.

Pleasure, food, drink, sex, drugs, money, power, prestige may be used responsibly, as was intended. Or they can grow into powerful addictions.

Most of us aren't called to be ascetics. But we do run the risk of having an enjoyment take control of our lives. If we can admit that we're becoming too dependent on something or someone, we have taken the first step towards eliminating needless pain from our lives.

— *Christophers*

To Family, Friends, Others. . .

• Call before you visit; say how long you will stay. Sense when not to visit. As a rule, make visits short. Be alert to signs of fatigue or pain.

• Sit down. Get at eye level, touch, establish real contact. Listen. Even a short visit will have more meaning.

• Anticipation is important. Send something regularly: a note, a card, a prayer, bits of humor or odd information clipped from a newspaper. But remember, your presence, when appropriate, is your best gift to a patient.

• Be authentic in what you say. Avoid false cheeriness or empty words. Saying "You look great" to a person suffering in body or spirit is brushing aside his pain. A hug or a pat on the arm may say all that needs to be said.

• Offer specific help to the patient or family: baby-sitting, an errand, a ride.

• Avoid criticism of the care the patient is receiving. It can be upsetting.

• Let the patient guide you in his or her needs and wants instead of imposing your own ideas. Ask, "What would you like me to do for you?" Be available.
• Let the patient give you something, however small or intangible.
• Treat the patient as a person, not an illness. Be aware, as a doctor, or nurse, that use of a patient's first name can be diminishing.
• Let a dying patient find the release of entering into all his or her feelings and unfinished business. Those close can help the patient to let his or her life go.

"Pray for one another that you may be healed." (James 5:15)

— *Christophers*

The End of the Day, Sally James Farnham. Courtesy of Brookgreen Gardens. Photo: Bobby Phillips.

Give sorrow words; the grief that does not speak
Whispers that o'er frought heart and bids it
    break.
— *William Shakespeare, (Macbeth)*

Crossing The Bar

Sunset and evening star,
And one clear call for me!
And may there be no moaning of the bar,
When I set out to sea.

But such a tide as moving seems asleep,
Too full for sound and foam,
When that which drew from out the boundless deep
Turns again home.

Twilight and evening bell,
And after that the dark!
And may there be no sadness of farewell;
When I embark;

For tho' from out our bourne of Time and Place,
The flood may bear me far,
I hope to see my Pilot face to face,
When I have crossed the bar.

— *Alfred Lord Tennyson*

—◄•••►—

She Loved Flowers:
Being A Story For A Mountain Lady

It was in the spring, the spring of 1874, as close as I can figure. Up near the head of Yancey Cove, young Mary and her Joe had sheared their little flock of sheep.

And the lambs kicked and jumped and looked so funny as Mary worked through that pile of smelly wool, picking out the briars and burrs, keeping her eyes all the time on her two little girls—married just three years now she was, and already a hip baby and a lap baby to tend.

She must have smiled as she worked, maybe thinking about life and how Joe had pressed his hard body close to her in their rope-sprung bed the night before; how his rough hands had been a comfort; how he had put a bunch of fresh wildflowers on the table that morning where she would find them, first thing.

Spring came on full and hot that year as she worked up that sheep wool. In between helping Joe in the steep fields, she would wash the fleece, again and again, until that pile of wool was as clean as creekwater and lye soap could make it.

Then she would sit carding wool in the quiet of the summer evenings, family fed, chores done. Maybe she hummed little tunes to herself and wondered if she should tell Joe about the winter baby a'comin, what with the crops a'failing and him being so moody about the money they owed.

By the time the wool was ready to spin, there was nothing left to say about the winter baby. Joe would put his hand on her proud belly, there where it pushed at the top of her apron. He would smile and say maybe it would be a boy this time. His mountain woman probably just sighed, and put her sunbrown hand on top of his.

Mary's feet and legs must have hurt right much that fall. You can't sit down to spin wool like you can with flax, least of all when you are big with child. So she stood and hurt and spun while the leaves turned red and gold and brown.

They didn't make much corn that fall and Joe had to sell the yearlings. He went to town to pay hard money on the loan interest and he came home drunk and quarrelsome. There were hard words, some his, some hers, and he left, mad and crazy-talking and he didn't come home for three days.

Afterwards, Mary would catch him looking off down the valley and rubbing at the beard-stubble on his face. Winter was a'coming; her baby was a'coming and her Joe could not make his mind stay at home.

They took Thanksgiving dinner at her mother's house. When they headed back up the holler, the big loom near about filled the wagon.

Mary got out and walked, there where the road was the roughest. She must have thought about how she looked, being so big, rar'd back and a'balancing. But it being nearly her time, and birthin' being so hard for her, she didn't want to take chances.

Joe set up the loom next to the fireplace. Mary measured off the wool and reeled it. Then she started in to tying up the heddles, winding shuttles and setting the pedals.

Back and forth the shuttle flew. Pedals rocked, beater down and back, set the ratchet. Lamplight and firelight, hour by hour, day by day until, halfway through December, she had two strips of wool cloth, each 30 inches wide and longer than Joe was tall. She hemmed and seamed them together and made her a blanket. Then she folded it away in the dovetailed chest.

Christmas came and went. She laughed and frolicked with the girls. There was an orange and three pieces of peppermint candy for each of them and the two caps that their Grandma had knit. When she opened the Bible to read the Christmas story, the wildflowers she had pressed that spring slipped from the pages and fell, pale and fluttery, to the floor.

And the wind blew New Year's Day past their cabin door while winter kept them house-bound.

Mary's time came on Old Christmas, before day. She sat up shock-straight in bed with a hard cramping pain shooting through her belly. She told Joe to go for Granny Meadows, real fast now, because the baby was coming on quick.

Granny Meadows came. She did all she knew and delivered the baby, but Mary set in to bleeding and it wouldn't stop even when the granny woman whispered the words out of the Bible that are supposed to stop the blood.

Mary smiled a little when they told her it was a boy-child. She said to name it Jim, after Joe's daddy. Joe sat beside her and held her hand while they covered her and tried to keep her warm with soapstones and hot irons. They tried, but it was no use, for the last words she ever said were, "Joe, Joe, I'm so cold."

And Mary, the wife of Joe, the mother of three, died, lacking only four days of being 19 years old.

They chipped out a hole in the frozen ground and buried her up on the hill, with all her kin. They wrapped the baby in Mary's new blanket and took him and the two girls to live with their Grandma and Grandpa.

Joe wouldn't stay. He had to go back to the cabin he had built for Mary and carve out the letters for her stone, one by one.

> Mary, Wife To Joe
> Mother To Sally, Mae, Jim
> Born Jan. 11, 1856
> Died Jan. 7, 1875
> Gone to Live with God
> She Loved Flowers

Spring came and Joe planted the stone. Then he went to the woods and picked wildflowers to leave in a bunch with Mary, on the hill, because she loved flowers.

The children stayed with Mary's family while Joe went off to work in a logging camp. Last anybody heard, he was working out in Oregon. He quit writing after a while. Nobody ever knew why.

The girls and the baby Jim grew up, married, had babies of their own, and died. And the years slipped by, pale and fluttery, like pressed wildflowers slipping from the pages of a book.

One day, 11 years ago, Jim's grandchildren gathered up some things to take to town to sell on Trade Day. One thing they found was a thin old blanket of cream-colored wool.

I saw the blanket on their table. I asked if it was for sale. They said yes, that it was, for 12 dollars. I said it was handmade and asked if they knew. They said yes, they knew, because Great-Grandmother Mary had wove it before she died.

I asked if they were bound to sell it. They said things like that didn't mean a lot these days and they could use the money. Anyways, it was scratchy and not nearly as warm as the ones from Sears.

So I bought it, then I sat a while with them and they told me the story about Joe, Mary, Jim and the girls.

I love that old blanket. I love to touch it and feel the twists from the spinning and the rough and wandering loom edges. Where the seam runs up the middle, I once thought I saw a tiny rust-red spot where Mary must have pricked her finger with the needle as she sewed her short days to her long nights in December, 1874.

And I think about how Mary is no kin to me or you, but how that she is kin to all of us. Young Mary, sunlight sifting through her hair, wildflowers at her feet, loved and loving; is a weathered stone on a hillside; family memories in her great-grandchildren's minds; and a blanket that she wove just before she died, lacking only four days being 19 years old.

So I give you Mary's blanket, a gift of Christmastime. Cherish it as I have cherished it; love it for all the reasons that we hill-born folk love our wrinkled land. A mountain woman wove Mary's blanket. Now I give it to you, mountain lady. Hold it in trust—for all of us.

— *Zack Allen, (The Asheville, Citizen)*

The Troubled Can Overcome Breaking Points

Everybody sooner or later reaches the breaking point. That is the place where desperation replaces reason and you feel you cannot go on. Some people get there often, for they live close to it: they may even reside on the edge of the abyss. Others have only heard about it so far, or may have seen it only once in their whole lives. But late or soon, infrequently or often, we all get there.

. . . However, everybody has his breaking point, an end to his rope. And when you get there you will likely ask for God's help. If you are really there, so will He be. God will work with us. He will supply our lack. He will comfort the comfortless, bind up the wounds of the broken-hearted, and supply His grace to those who are at the breaking point.

— *L.D. Johnson, Furman University Chaplain*

Old Clinchfield Railroad Built
By Wild, Death-Dealing Crews

Little Switzerland, N.C.

A steadily mounting number of hastily dug graves along the right of way, few of which are now identifiable, marked the progress of the roadbed for the Clinchfield Railroad after the work of extending it over and through the steep, confused mountain ridges south of Spruce Pine was begun in the spring of 1905.

Reid Queen, Sr., now 72, who a few years later was to become Little Switzerland's first postmaster, worked as a pipe fitter on the miles of steam lines supplying power to drill the holes for the tons of dynamite which were required to blast through mile after mile of solid rock.

He vividly recalls some of the violent deaths that befell unfortunate laborers through explosions, cave-ins and other accidents and by pistols or knives wielded by their fellow workers.

No record is now available, if one was ever kept, of the total number of lives lost in various disasters and through exposure, the ravages of disease and other causes; but 20 miles of railroad between Spruce Pine and

Marion were probably the most costly—both in lives and money—ever completed in the South.

17 Tunnels Blasted

In these 20 miles the roadbed descends more than 1,000 feet. To achieve a reasonable grade it was necessary to blast some 17 tunnels, ranging from a few hundred feet to nearly a quarter of a mile in length. Even with the cheap labor then available, one stretch of road is said to have cost as much as $1,000,000 a mile.

Self-propelled earth and rock moving machinery had not then come into use. Except for blasting, and mule-drawn carts and dragpans, the Herculean task was accomplished with manual labor. More than 3,000 laborers and 200 mules were in use at one time.

Italians, Germans, and Russians were recruited in northern cities, many just off boats in New York. Few had little, if any knowledge of English. The construction company had to employ an interpreter, who was kept busy going up and down the line from one to another of the seven labor camps to help settle disputes and explain various matters to the immigrants. Some native labor was also employed and a number of Negroes were brought in.

These construction years were the most turbulent this area has ever known. With such an admixture of racial backgrounds and temperaments, with the laborers crowded into tiny tar-paper shacks lining the muddy, rock camp "streets," anything could happen—and often did. Innumerable fights and sometimes murder were natural results.

Reid Queen says the laborers had to prepare their own food, purchased from the camp commissaries. He recalls that at one camp some 15 Italians employed one of their countrymen as a cook. One evening when they returned from work to find their cook drunk and no signs of supper being prepared, there was an explosion of Italian temperament, for this evidently was the climax of a long series of such derelictions on the part of the cook.

Trial Held

"They sobered the fellow up and held a trial according to their own law," says Queen, "and the poor man was sentenced to be tied to a tree and shot. The sentence was promptly executed."

Later, says Queen, this group of Italians stood trial in Raleigh for murder. Four or five of them were sentenced to prison terms ranging from 5 to 10 years.

Queen also recalls the time a camp superintendent named Kidd from Kentucky was shot in the back by the brother of a workman he was mistreating, and the brother in turn shot by a friend of Kidd's. Both bodies fell into the doorway of a shanty before which they had been standing. Kidd's friend fled the scene but was later caught in Marion, tried for murder, and sentenced to seven years in prison.

Queen says that one day he was eye witness to the murder of a Negro laborer by another member of his race. This happened near Snipes Tunnel and Camp No. 4, where Mt. Mitchell station was later established. Name of the Station was subsequently changed to Little Switzerland, and several years ago was abandoned except as a flag stop.

Queen and one of his helpers were at a spring adjusting the flow of water for the row of coal-fired boilers down at the camp when they heard a noise and looked up to see a Negro running at breakneck speed. A few moments later another Negro came plunging down the mountainside after him with a pistol in his hand. The pursuer fired one shot and his victim fell dead. The murderer kept running and, as far as Queen could learn, was never apprehended.

Razor Battle

Queen also recalls that at one of the camps a fight between two Negro women resulted in one of them being so badly slashed with a razor that she quickly bled to death. Queen says the murderess was sentenced to serve 20 years which later was commuted to 10.

Queen also remembers the day a gang was working at the base of a 30-foot cut when the upper part of the bank suddenly caved in, burying alive seven men beneath tons of loose dirt and rock. All were from the Bear Creek section of Mitchell County.

On that same day, Queen says nine more workers were killed in upper Bridle Path Tunnel by an explosion resulting from careless handling of dynamite. Some 13 cases containing 100 pounds of dynamite each, had been carted several hundred feet into the tunnel, where drilling for a fresh blast had just been completed. It was later reported that a worker had been using a long sharp rock "about the size of a man's shoe" to knock the tops off the heavy wooden cases.

Suddenly the mountain was shaken by a terrific detonation. When the tunnel could be entered after the dust and fumes of the explosion had cleared away the bodies of only three of the nine laborers—a Russian and two Negros—could be found. Remains of the other six workers were splattered all over the rocky walls of the tunnel.

Riot Occurs

There was also the riot at Camp No. 6, led by an Italian named Jimmy Mazone. Five "Tallies," as the native workers called them, were killed and were "buried under the chestnut by the Honeycutt Tunnel, all lying in a row." But there were others—just how many was not reported at the time—whose bodies "in a gully, lying all torn and mixed up" were not discovered until buzzards were observed wheeling above the spot.

The death toll continued to mount until the way through the Blue Ridge was cleared and the first train ran to Marion in 1908. The late James A. Mayberry of Spruce Pine often told of riding in 1910 on the first passenger train to enter Spartanburg, S.C., southern terminus of the Clinchfield. At that time many of the graves along the right of way between Spruce Pine and Marion were still in evidence.

— Ashton Chapman

Admitting Vulnerability

A dying man asked the newly graduated nurse to talk with him. "I can't," she said. "I'm too afraid." Her candor elicited his reassurance that what she said didn't matter. She learned that it was enough just to sit with him.

— The Christophers

End of the Trail, James Earle Fraser. Courtesy of Brookgreen
Gardens.

> An infant crying in the night;
> An infant crying for the light;
> And with no language but a cry.
> — *Alfred Lord Tennyson*

Despair

Few people have lived very long without at some time experiencing the feeling of despair. At some brief period in our lives, perhaps only hope kept us from self-destruction. To nourish such feeling is the ultimate tragedy in this life. If we are to survive we must attach ourselves to something stronger than ourselves—ultimately, only God has such power.

The moving finger writes, and having writ
Moves on; nor all your piety nor wit
Shall lure it back to cancel half a line,
Nor all your tears wash out a word of it.
— *Omar Khayyam, (Rubaiyat)*

Will all great Neptune's ocean wash this blood clean
    from my hand? No, this my hand will rather
The multitudinous seas incarnadine,
Making the green one red.
From this instant
There's nothing serious in mortality,
All but toys; renown and grace is dead;
The wine of life is drawn, and the mere lees
I left this vault to brag of.
— *William Shakespeare, (Macbeth)*

173

To be, or not to be,—that is the question:—
Whether 'tis nobler in the mind, to suffer
The slings and arrows of outrageous fortune;
Or to take arms against a sea of troubles,
And, by opposing, end them?—to die,—to sleep,—
No more;—and, by a sleep, to say we end
The heartache, and the thousand natural shocks
That flesh is heir to,—'tis a consummation
Devoutly to be wish'd, To die;—to sleep:—
To sleep! perchance to dream;—ay there's the rub;
For in that sleep of death what dreams may come,
When we have shuffled off this moral coil,
Must give us pause: There's the respect,
That makes calamity of so long life:
For who would bear the whips and scorns of time,
The oppressor's wrong, the proud man's contumely,
The pangs of despis'd love,
The law's delay
The insolence of office. . .
To grunt and sweat under a weary life!
But that the dread of something after death,—
The undiscover'd country, from whose bourn
No traveler returns,—puzzles the will;
And makes us rather bear those ills we have,
Than fly to others that we know not of?
Thus conscience does make cowards of us all; . . .
                    — *William Shakespeare, (Hamlet)*

"Mark Twain" was the pen name of Samuel Clemens, who as a young man fell in love with a beautiful Christian girl by the name of Livy and married her. Being devoted to her Lord before marriage, she was interested in having a family altar and prayer at meals after she and Sam were married. This was done for a time, and then one day Samuel Clemens said, "Livy, you can go on with this by yourself if you want to, but leave me out. I don't believe in your God and you're only making a hypocrite of me."

Fame and wealth came. There were court appearances in Europe. Sam and Livy were riding high for the time being, and Livy got further and further away from her early devotion to her Lord. The eventual fall came. In an hour of bitter need Sam Clemens said, "Livy, if your Christian faith can help you any now, turn to it." Livy replied, "I can't, Sam, I haven't any. It was destroyed a long time ago."

— *Author unknown*

Tomorrow, and, tomorrow, and tomorrow,
Creeps in this petty place from day to day
To the last syllable of recorded time,
And all our yesterdays have lighted fools
The way to dusty death. Out, out, brief candle!
Life's but a walking shadow, a poor player
That struts and frets his hour upon the stage
And then is heard no more; it is a tale
Told by an idiot, full of sound and fury,
Signifying nothing. . . .

I am sick at heart—
I have lived long enough; my way of life
Has fallen into the sear, the yellow leaf;
And that which should accompany old age,
Like honor, love, obedience, troops of friends,
I must not look to have; but in their stead,
Curses, not loud but deep, mouth-honor, breath,
Which the poor heart would fain deny, but dare not. . . .

Me thought I heard a voice cry, "Sleep no more!"
Macbeth doth murder sleep, the innocent sleep,
Sleep that knits up the raveled sleeve of care,
The death of each day's life, sore labor's bath,
Balm of hurt minds, great nature's second course,
Chief nourishes in life's feast. . .
Macbeth shall sleep no more!. . .
Go get some water, and wash this filthy witness from
    your hand.

— *William Shakespeare, (Macbeth)*

Fatigue, Cecil Howard. Courtesy of Brookgreen Gardens.

Life's but a walking shadow, a poor player
That struts and frets his hour upon the stage
And then is heard no more; it is a tale
Told by an idiot full of sound and fury,
Signifying nothing. . .
　　　　　　— *William Shakespeare, (Macbeth)*

*Man was not created to be sufficient unto himself
and his mind is finite. God gave man dominion over
all he had made except over himself; He kept man to
have fellowship with Him and dependent upon Him.
Man endeavors to live independently of his Maker only
at his own peril. "Invictus" with all its beauty is fraught
with tragedy and final despondence.*

— *R.B. Phillips*

Invictus

Out of the night that covers me,
Black as the pit from pole to pole,
I thank whatever gods may be,
For my unconquerable soul.

In the fell clutch of circumstance
I have not winched nor cried aloud.
Under the bludgeonings of chance
My head is bloody but unbowed.

Beyond the place of wrath and tears
Looms but the horror of the shade,
And yet, the menacing of the years,
Finds, and shall find me, unafraid.

— *W. Ernest Henley*

The mass of men lead lives of quiet desperation.
What is called resignation is confirmed desperation. From
the desperate city you go to the desperate country, and
have to console yourself with the bravery of minks and
muskrats. A stereotyped but unconscious despair is concealed even under what are called the games and amuse-
ments of mankind. There is no play in them, for this
comes after work. But it is a characteristic of wisdom not
to do desperate things.

— *Henry D. Thoreau*

He [Judas] then having received the sop went immediately out: and it was night.

— John 13:30

—————

Lady Macbeth (walking in her sleep, washing her hands):
. . . Out, damned spot! Out I say. . . what, will these
    hands ne'er be cleaned?. . .
Here's the smell of blood still: all the perfumes of Arabia
    will not sweeten this little hand! Oh, oh, oh!
. . . Wash your hands, put on your nightgown: Look not
    so pale.
. . . To bed, to bed!
There's a knocking at the gate;
Come, come, come, come, give me your hand.
What's done cannot be undone. . . to bed, to bed, to
    bed. . .
Doctor: More needs she the divine than the physician.

— William Shakespeare, (Macbeth)

—————

Benediction, Daniel Chester French. Courtesy of Brookgreen Gardens.

Lord, make me an instrument of thy peace.
— *St. Francis of Assisi*

COMFORT

No matter how bravely we try to act there are times in every life when we desperately need to be comforted by someone or some power outside ourselves.

If we are not to despair we must be comforted. Comfort renews hope; without hope we lack desire to live.

———————

O, the comfort, the inexpressible comfort, of feeling safe with a person, having neither to weigh thoughts, nor measure words, but pouring them all out, just as they are, chaff and grain together; Certain that a faithful hand will take and sift them, keep that which is worth keeping, and with a breath of kindness, blow the rest away.

— *Eric Fromm*

———————

The Lord bless thee, and keep thee:
The Lord make his face shine upon thee, and be gracious unto thee:
The Lord lift up his countenance upon thee, and give thee peace.

— *Numbers 6:24–26*

For I am persuaded that neither death, nor life, nor angels, nor principalities, nor powers, nor things present, nor things to come,

Nor height, nor depth, nor any other creature, shall be able to separate us from the love of God, which is in Christ Jesus our Lord.

— Romans 8:38–39

Truth forever on the scaffold, wrong forever on the
   throne. . .
Yet that scaffold sways the future, and, behind the dim
   unknown,
Standeth God within the shadow, keeping watch above
   his own.

— Author unknown

The Northeaster, Winslow Homer. The Brooklyn Museum.

He arose,
He spake,
He gave command;
He rebuked the winds and the sea—
So that the storm became at once as silent as a whisper.

— R.B. Phillips

The Storm

From the soft sweet waters of the Sea of Galilee
He sailed in a small boat with twelve of his chosen men.
Soon a great storm arose and dashed the craft at will;
Like a toy thrown aside by a restless child.
It fought the wanton sea until all hope was gone.
"Lo," said one, "why fear the angry waves?
When near, in the hold of the ship,
Lies the Maker of earth, and sky, and sea?
Why struggle within ourselves, when all is vain?

"Behold the Son of God, the Maker of earth, and sky,
    and sea,
Is waiting for our request to give command
To all that was, and is, and is to be,
If we will trust His will."
He arose,
He spake,
He gave command;
He rebuked the winds and the sea,
And there was a great calm;
So that the storm became at once as silent as a whisper.
A great shout arose among the men:
"What manner of man is this that even the winds and
    the sea obey Him?"

How many times have we, his children, been tossed
With broken hearts on life's mad and restless sea!
Searching in vain for the when, and where, and how of
    life!
Facing the "slings and arrows of outrageous fortune,
Taking up arms against a sea of trouble!"
When just beside us, even within us,
Lies all power on earth, and sky, and sea;
The touch of his hand ready and eager to lift us
Beyond all harm!
What manner of man is this that even the winds and sea
    obey Him!

— R.B. Phillips

Comfort

Don't you know by now that the everlasting God,
The creator of the farthest parts of the earth
Never grows faint or weary?
No one can fathom the depths of his understanding.
He gives power to the tired and worn out,
And strength to the weak.
Even the youths shall be exhausted,
And the young men will all give up.
But they that wait upon the Lord
Shall renew their strength.
They shall mount up with wings like eagles;
They shall run and not be weary;
They shall walk and not faint.
— *Isaiah 41:28–30, (Living Bible)*

Dr. Peter Marshall, once U.S. Chaplain, sat eating a meal with a minister friend who asked him this searching question: "Peter, you know you are an imperfect human being, live in a world of sin, and have at some time broken God's laws. At the final judgment what shall you say to the Father when he reminds you of your sins?"

Silent for a moment, he replied, "I shall not worry about that, John, for by my side Jesus will be standing, and will lay his hand on my shoulder and say, 'Father, this is one of my boys.' "
— *R.B. Phillips*

If something worries me, I think of God;
If someone is unkind to me, I think of God;
If I should come face to face with death or disaster,
I should think of God.
— *Roger Babson*

In about the year 120 A.D., Pliny, the Roman governor of Bythynia, was trying to root out Christianity. Of
course, to do so he had to root out Christians. He said to
one great soul, "I will kill you"

And the answer came, "You cannot, for my life is
hidden with Christ in God."

"I will take away your treasures."

And again the great soul replied, "You cannot, for
my treasures are in heaven."

"I will drive you away from me, and you shall not
have a friend left."

The Christian replied, "You cannot, for I have a
Friend from whom you cannot separate me."

— *Author unknown*

Photo: Bobby Phillips.
And this our life, exempt from public haunt,
Finds tongues in trees, books in running brooks, sermons in
    stones
And good in everything.
I would not change it.

— *William Shakespeare, (As You Like It)*

In Temptation

Jesus, lover of my soul,
    Let me to thy bosom fly,
While the nearer waters roll,
    While the tempest still is high!
Hide me, O my Savior, hide,
    Till the storm of life is past,
Safe into the haven guide;
    O receive my soul at last!

— Charles Wesley

Child's Evening Prayer

Now I lay my weary head
Upon the pillow of my bed.
I thank you, Father, for this day,
And what it's meant in work and play.
For mother dear and father too,
And loving friends so good and true.
Before I close my eye in sleep,
I give myself to you to keep.
I know, my Lord, I am so small,
And yet to thee I give it all.
Keep me through another night,
And let me see the morning light.
But if you do not leave me here,
I trust myself to Jesus' care.

— R.B. Phillips

Thou wilt keep him in perfect peace, whose mind is stayed on thee.

— Isaiah 26:3

For he shall give his angels charge over thee, to keep thee in all thy ways.

— Psalms 91:11

Trust in the Lord with all your heart, and lean not on your own understanding. In all thy ways acknowledge him, and he shall direct thy paths.

— Proverbs 3:5–6

Cast all your fears on him, for he careth for you.

— I Peter 5:7

For we know all things work for good to those that love God, to them who are called according to his purpose.

— Romans 8:28

With thoughtless and impatient hands
We tangle up the plans
The Lord hath wrought!
And when we cry in pain
He sayeth, "Be quiet dear
While I untie the knot."

— Author unknown

Behold, I stand at the door, and knock: if any man
hear my voice, and open the door, I will come in to him,
and will sup with him, and he with me.

— Revelation 3:20

I often think of how I'd got my fishing line all tangled
    up.
The more I pulled the worse it got.
Finally I'd hand the whole thing over to you,
And you'd smooth it out.
So I generally do that with my problems now,
And I'm trying not to pull the line much,
Before I give it to Him.

Arab, Allan Clark. Courtesy of Brookgreen Gardens. Photo:
Bobby Phillips.

The Lord is my strength,
And He will make my feet
like hind's feet,
And He will make me
To walk in my high places.
— Habakkak 3:19

Have you been pulling the line
With that problem that troubles you today?
Just hand it over to your Heavenly Father,
And see how swiftly and lovingly
He will untangle the criss-cross
And knotty impossibility
that have been troubling you so!

— Sunday School Times

A little Scotch girl was making a trip to London on one of Scotland's finest trains, the Flying Scotsman. Seated opposite her in the little compartment was a worldly-wise traveler. As the train gathered speed and rocked and swayed through the rugged mountains in the darkness of the night, he became quite nervous. Glancing across at the little girl, he noticed that she was entirely undisturbed.

"Young lady," said the traveler, "aren't you just a little bit scared?" "No, sir," she replied.

"Then tell me, why aren't you scared?" her companion inquired.

"Because my father is the engineer of this train," she quietly answered, "and I just know he won't let anything happen to us."

— Author unknown

And I said to the man who stood at the gate of the year: "Give me a light that I may tread safely into the unknown." And he replied, "Go out into the darkness and put your hand into the hand of God. That shall be better than a light, and better than a safer way."

— M.L. Haskins

The Meeting

Men made me dread to meet God. . . but I found it
    sweet. . . .
I who had disobeyed the laws men said he made.
Yet from Him was no "You! You wretch for mercy sue!
You wicked sinner!" Rather, just like a gentle Father,
"Son, how your garden grows! I love that yellow rose.
And that narcissus seems to come from the land of
    dreams.
For the fine work you've done, I'm proud of you, dear
    Son."

— Archibald Rutledge

The Marshes of Glynn

As the marsh-hen secretly builds on the watery sod,
Behold I will build me a nest on the greatness of God:
I will fly in the greatness of God as the marsh-hen flies.
In the freedom that fills all the space twixt the marsh
    and the skies;
By so many roots as the marsh grass sends into the sod
I will heartily lay me a hold on the greatness of God:
Oh, like the greatness of God is the greatness within
The range of the marshes, the liberal marshes of Glynn.

— Sidney Lanier

Lead, Kindly Light

Lead, Kindly Light, amid the encircling gloom,
    Lead thou me on!
The night is dark, and I am far from home—
    Lead thou me on!
Keep thou my feet; I do not ask to see
The distant scene—one step enough for me.

I was not ever thus, nor prayed that Thou
    Shouldst lead me on.
I loved to choose and see my path; but now
    Lead thou me on!

I loved the garish day, and, spite of fears,
Pride ruled my will; remember not past years.

So long thy power hath blessed me, sure it still
    Will lead me on,
O'er moor and fen, o'er crag and torrent, till
    The night is gone;
And with the morn those angel faces smile
Which I have loved long since, and lost awhile.
           — *Cardinal John Henry Newman*

Let not your heart be troubled: ye believe in God,
believe also in me.
              — *John 14:1*

Praying Hands.
I will lift up my eyes unto the hills, from whence
cometh my help.
              — *Psalm 121:1*

Forest Idyl, Aalbin Polasek. Courtesy of Brookgreen Gardens.

    The quality of mercy is not strained
It droppeth as the gentle rain from heaven
Upon the place beneath. . .
— *William Shakespeare, (Merchant of Venice)*

FORGIVENESS AND MERCY

There is no way for a person to be reasonably happy without the spirit of forgiveness. Nobody ever lives many years without the need to forgive and to be forgiven. There is no way to avoid the destructive forces on body and mind caused by an unforgiving spirit.

Such a spirit corrodes the life of all parties concerned. Sometimes we try to justify ourselves by "you don't know what he did to me!" No matter what he did to me, I must forgive if I'm to have any health or peace of mind.

We have no right to ask God to forgive us until we have forgiven others. "Forgive us our trespasses as we forgive others their trespasses" is found in The Lord's Prayer.

General Grant was reputed to have asked Lincoln what should be done with Jefferson Davis, to which Abe replied, "If you can let Jeff Davis escape please do so because I don't want him."

Prophetic religion through the ages has stressed the need for forgiveness and tolerance . . . psychology now supplements this insight by teaching us that we can achieve inner health only through forgiveness—the forgiveness not only of others but also of ourselves. . . .

— *Joshua Liebman*

193

Words Written In A Concentration Camp

When a Nazi concentration camp was liberated, this prayer by a Jew was found on a scrap of paper:

Peace be to men of bad will, and an end to all revenge to all words of pain and punishment.. . .

So many have borne witness with their blood!

O God, do not put their suffering upon the scales of Thy justice,

Lest it be counted to the hangman, lest he be brought to answer for his atrocities.

But to all hangmen and informers, to all traitors and evil ones, do grant the benefit of the courage and fortitude shown by those others, who were their victims.. . .

Grant the benefit of the burning love and sacrifice in those harrowed, tortured hearts, which remained strong and steadfast in the face of death and unto their weakest hour.

All this, O Lord, may it count in Thine eyes, so that their sin be forgiven.

May this be the ransom that restores justice.

And all that is good, let it be counted, and all that is evil, let it be wiped out.. . .

May peace come once more upon this earth, peace to men of good will; and may it descend upon the others also. Amen.   — *from* Dimanche, *a French weekly*

The Muddy Boots

A hard-boiled Army sergeant walked down the aisle in a little church, gave his heart to Christ, and gave his testimony to the audience.

He said that one single event had led to his decision. In the barracks where he slept, there was an overgrown private who was deeply religious. Every night before piling into his bunk, the private would get down on his knees and pray. The sergeant didn't like it. One evening he raised up in his own bed, picked up his muddy boots lying on the floor, and hurled one at the praying soldier, striking him on the head and stunning him for a few painful moments.

"The next morning," said the sergeant, "I reached for my muddy boots. There they were—all cleaned and polished! Later, I found that the praying private had done that for me. I just couldn't take it. It finally drove me to seek the One who could make a man like that."

— Sunday School Teacher

Forgiveness Is . . .

Forgiveness is a decision
Forgiveness is showing mercy even when the injury has
    been deliberate.
Forgiveness is accepting the person as he is.
Forgiveness is taking a risk.
Forgiveness is accepting an apology.
Forgiveness is a way of living.
Forgiveness is choosing to love.

— The Christophers

"Live together in the forgiveness of your sins for without it no human fellowship . . . can survive. Don't insist on your rights, don't blame each other, don't judge or condemn each other, don't find fault with each other, but take one another as you are, and forgive each other every day from the bottom of your hearts."

— Dietrich Bonhoeffer

The Christ of the Andes, (a 20-foot statue of Christ) was erected in 1904 at the conclusion of a peaceful settlement of a dangerous quarrel between Argentina and Chile. It was placed on the boundary between the two countries. On it is carved this inscription:

Sooner shall these mountains crumble into dust than Argentina and Chile shall violate the peace they have pledged at the feet of Christ the Savior.

— *Author unknown*

Christ of the Andes, Mateo Alonzo. Photo: Burton Holmes.

Lord, make me an instrument of thy peace. Where there is hatred, let me sow love; where there is injury, pardon; where there is doubt, faith; where there is despair, hope; where there is darkness, light; where there is sadness, joy. O Divine Master, grant that I may not so much seek to be consoled as to console; to be understood as to understand; to be loved, as to love.

— *St. Francis of Assisi*

The quality of mercy is not strain'd;
It droppeth as the gentle rain from heaven
Upon the place beneath; it is twice blest:
It blesseth him that gives, and his that takes.
'Tis mightiest in the mightiest; it becomes
The throned monarch better than his crown. . .
Is it enthroned in the hearts of kings,
It is an attribute to God himself;
And earthly power doth then show likest God's
When mercy seasons justice.

— *William Shakespeare, (Merchant of Venice)*

John Newton was born in London in 1725. Having only a meager opportunity at home, he ran away to sea in his early years. By his own confession he walked the ways of darkest sin, being engaged in the African slave trade, a dealer in human flesh, and an infidel. He was born again in a storm at sea, and it was he who wrote:

"Amazing grace! how sweet the sound,
That saved a wretch like me!
I once was lost, but now am found,
Was blind, but now I see."

— *R.B. Phillips*

A Plea For Mercy

A recent discovery of a letter in an old store account book belonging to my uncle, Sam J. Ford, and written by his wife, Laura Phillips Ford, discloses clearly what it means for one to have love, compassion, mercy, and unlimited faith in God. This letter is copied here in full.

— *R.B. Phillips*

Ledger, June 27, 1891

To the Bakersville, North Carolina, Lodge No. 357 Brothers one and all:

I call you brothers, not as the wife of a Mason, but as a daughter of a Mason and sister of Masons.

This is a very solemn morning with me when I see Masons and the friends of Masonry making their way to the great and grand celebration, and my husband, who loves Masonry and loves his family, is deprived of this great privilege.

Not that I censure the Lodge for anything they have done in the matter, but that as good a man as my husband to have the misfortune of giving over to strong drink.

Now I write this only to give you all a correct history of my husband. He is now letting liquor of all kinds alone; and I believe he is trying to seek that peace with God that has promised that His Grace is sufficient for all crises. He has taken me and his little boys upstairs, where none but God could see, and asked us to kneel with him, and that we might all ask God to give him grace to overcome strong drink; and that he might be a sober father and sober husband.

Some of you may not know my husband's disposition. I will give it in short. He is a man that loves Sunday Schools. To prove that to you, he has been in 50 Sundays out of 52; he would have put in the other two but he was away from home. He is now a regular scholar when he does not go off to preaching somewhere. He paid $1.00 out of his own pocket for literature this year, it being one third the cost of it. I never knew him to fail helping to raise money and putting some in advance to God's cause. He feeds all ministers and says he would rather they would stay with him than any other class of people. He won't sell his fruit and grain to make liquor. He gave a choice building spot of his land for a church seat, and $50.00 to start one. After that he gave nearly $25.00 more, and begged for money and subscriptions.

You, Bakersville Brothers, will know he is a good, kind husband to me, and a good and kind father to his children; he has them to read God's Word that they may become familiar with His good news and truth. I ask you to consider his case prayerfully, and if consistent with your wishes, to restore him again. He is not a bad man, and I am well acquainted with him. Help me to save him! My God knows the prayers I have offered up that he might quit drink. Please don't slight him, but give him your helping hand. I have seen him weep bitterly over distressed friends, financially and physically. The only thing I know against him is in the past. He has drunk too much whiskey, you all know.

How many of you will promise me that every morning of your life that you will go down on your knees to God and ask Him to give my husband grace to overcome strong drink? I think this is worth your notice. Outside of drink, how many are more worthy than he is; who pays more to the support of the gospel according to his wealth than he does? He works against liquor and advises all boys to let it alone. He does all he can to improve the stock of his country.

I hope none of you will take exception to this letter, read it and remember that it is from the hand of one that loves and fears God and is trying to get to heaven, and take all I can with me.

May God bless your Lodge and help you to reform and save many is my prayer.

Yours,
(Mrs.) L. V. Ford

Lincoln's Second Inaugural

With malice toward none; and charity for all
With firmness in the right, as God gives us to see the
   right,
Let us strive to finish the work we are in;
To bind up the nation's wounds,
To care for him who shall have borne the battle,
And for his widow and his orphans—
To do all which may achieve and cherish
A just and lasting peace
Among ourselves and among all nations.

— Abraham Lincoln, arranged by R.B. Phillips

Carl Sandburg, distinguished biographer of Abraham Lincoln, said that in Lincoln's day it was a custom for political opponents to engage in joint debate. On one occasion in a town just outside of Springfield, Abe traveled in his opponent's carriage.

After his opponent had spoken Abe arose to say, "I am too poor to own a carriage, but my opponent has generously invited me to ride with him. I want you to vote for me, if you will, but if not, then vote for my opponent, for he is a fine man."

— R.B. Phillips

If we discovered that we had only five minutes left to say all we wanted to say, every telephone booth would be occupied by people calling other people to stammer that they loved them. Why wait until the last five minutes?

— Christopher Morley

"Didn't this man you just spoke of do you great harm one time?"

"Yes, I distinctly remember forgetting about it years ago."

> — *Clara Barton, founder of the Red Cross*

———•◆◆•———

With malice toward none, and charity to all.

> — *Abraham Lincoln*

———•◆◆•———

Janet Phillips. Photo: Bobby Phillips.
> If I have freedom in my love
> And in my soul I am free,
> Angels alone, that soar above
> Enjoy such liberty.
> — *Richard Lovelace*

HAPPINESS

All normal people seem to seek happiness. Most of us believe it will come by gratification of physical senses. Happiness does not come by seeking it for ourselves, but rather as a result of what we think and do for others. It comes by the pursuit of worthy ideas and goals. Somebody has well said, "Happiness is the finding of God's will for our lives and doing it." Happiness is a cut above pleasure, but the two are practically synonymous.

———————

Peace I leave with you, my peace I give unto you; not as the world giveth, give I unto you. Let not your heart be troubled, neither let it be afraid.

— John 14:27

———————

"The earth hath he given to the children of men." *(Psalms 115:15)* What sort of world is ours?

1. It is a mad world. Mad men and women live in it. Men are made with hate, avarice, lust, ambition, and idolatry. Our world is full of madhouses with poor mad men and women in them. Old King Lear driven out in

203

the storm was mad; Lady Macbeth wringing her hands and pacing the floor was mad. We live in a mad world.

2. We live in a bad world. Bad men shoot one another, robbers murder one another. Bad men lead us into war and destroy the flower of a nation's youth. Bad thoughts, bad actions, bad living—this unwholesome triumvirate wrecks nations and destroys the body politic. It is a bad world we live in.

3. It is a sad world we live in. Broken-hearted women sit in the gloaming thinking of departed loved ones; a bright-eyed child of promise is taken and in the heart lingers the silence of a great hurt. The world is full of little children who are sad because they are poor and needy and homesick for mother. And how vacant, how sad, the lot of most people who have grown old! The very old are so often the very unhappy. The average man puts his best foot forward and appears happy to his fellows, but the average man is not happy. It is a sad world that you and I live in.

4. We live in a glad world where trees and flowers and birds make us glad. The hearts of men and women are made glad by the merry faces of little children. A good friend is like the shadow of a great rock in a weary land. The tender grace of a cool day brings with it beauty and gladness. This is a glad world you and I live in. The perfection of a rose, the beauty of a lily, the tenderness of a mother, the opportunity of doing some wonderful task that we love, the satisfaction of faith, the spring of hope, the privilege of knowing Christ, the prize at the end of the way—is it not a glad world after all?

— *Author unknown*

God grant me the Serenity to accept the things I cannot change, Courage to change the things I can, and Wisdom to know the difference.

— *Reinhold Niebuhr*

Those only are happy who have their minds on some object other than their own happiness; on the happiness of others, on the improvement of mankind, even on some art or pursuit, followed not as a means, but as itself an ideal end. Aiming thus at something else, they find happiness by the way.

— *John Stuart Mill*

Girl with Fish, H.R. Hyatt. Courtesy of Brookgreen Gardens.

Laughter is the music of the soul.

— *Irish Prayer*

We live in deeds, not years, in thoughts, not breaths
In feelings, not in figures on a dial.
We should count time by heart throbs.
He most lives who thinks most,
Feels the noblest, and acts the best.

— *Philip James Bailey*

To laugh often and much; to win the respect of intelligent people and the affection of children; to earn the appreciation of honest critics and endure the betrayal of false friends; to appreciate beauty, to find the best in others; to leave the world a bit better, whether by a healthy child, a garden patch, or a redeemed social condition; to know even one life has breathed easier because you lived. This is to have succeeded.

— *Ralph Waldo Emerson*

The purpose of life is not to be happy. The purpose of life is to matter, to be productive, to have it make some difference that you live at all. Happiness, in the ancient, noble verse, means self-fulfillment and is given to those who use to the fullest whatever talents God or luck or fate bestowed upon them.

— *Leo Rosten*

Pleasures are like poppies spread; you seize the flow'r, its bloom is dead.

— *Robert Burns*

If you tell the truth, you don't have to remember anything.

— *Mark Twain*

———◆◆◆———

If I had my life to live over again, I would make it a rule to read some poetry and listen to some music at least once every week; for perhaps the parts of my brain now atrophied would thus have been kept alive through use. The loss of these tastes is a loss of happiness.

— *Charles Darwin*

———◆◆◆———

If I can stop one heart from breaking,
I shall not live in vain;
If I can ease one life the aching,
Or cool one pain,
Or help one fainting robin
Into his nest again,
I shall not have lived in vain. . .

— *Emily Dickinson*

———◆◆◆———

I asked for strength that I might achieve; He made me weak that I might obey. I asked for health that I might do greater things. I asked for riches that I might be happy; I was given poverty that I might be wise. I asked for power that I might have the praise of men; I was given weakness that I might feel the need of God. I asked for all things that I might enjoy life; I was given life that I might enjoy all things. I received nothing that I asked for, all that I had hoped for. My prayer was answered.

— *Church Life*

The Art Of Happiness

You can't pursue happiness and catch it. Happiness comes upon you unawares while you are helping others. The philosophy of happiness is pointedly expressed in the old Hindu proverb, which reads: "Help thy brother's boat across, and lo! thine own has reached the shore."

Happiness does not depend upon a full pocketbook, but upon a full mind, of riches and thoughts and a heart full of rich emotions.

Happiness does not depend upon what happens outside of you but it is on what happens inside of you; it is measured by the spirit in which you meet the problems of life.

Happiness is a state of mind. Lincoln once said: "We are happy as we make up our minds to be."

Happiness does not come from doing easy work but from the afterglow of satisfaction that comes after the achievement of a difficult task, that demanded our best.

Happiness grows out of harmonious relationships with others, based on attitudes of good will, tolerance, understanding, and love.

Happiness is found in little things: a baby's smile, a letter from a friend, the song of a bird, a light in the window.

The master secret of happiness is to meet the challenge of each new day with the serene faith that: "All thing work together for good to them that love God."

— *Asheville, N.C., Police Department Youth Bureau*

———

I wonder how many of your readers would like to have the keys to true happiness? It is really so very simple:

If you know some who are hungry, give them to eat;

If you know someone destitute, comfort him or her;

If you know a stranger, welcome him or her;
If you know some who are thirsty, give them to drink;
If you know someone in prison, visit him or her.

For Christ said: "Each time that you do these things to the least of my brethren, you do them to me." He also said: "Each time that you neglect to do these things for one of these little ones you neglect to do them for me."

— *Author unknown*

Rearing Horses, F.W. MacMonnies. Courtesy of Brookgreen Gardens. Photo: Bobby Phillips
Be still and know that I am God.
— *Psalms 46:10*

Pleasures

We build air castles far and high;
We drink the passing pleasures full and free;
We soar above the mountains peaks—yet sigh;
For soon are pleasures gone from you and me.
To lasting peace, none has found the golden key;
Our joys but pay a hasty call and go;
With pain we buy each pleasure that we see;
To us, they come and go just like the snow—
They're fleeting, that is why we love them so.

— *R.B. Phillips*

Perhaps the human race has made some progress since the twelfth century.

— *R.B. Phillips*

Happiness lies in conquering one's enemies,
    in driving them in front of oneself, in
    taking their property, in
    savoring their despair, in
    outraging their wives and daughters.

— *Genghis Khan*

A Collect For Club Women

Keep us O God, from Pettiness; let us be large in thought,
    in word, in deed.
Let us be done with fault-finding and leave off self-
    seeking.
May we put away all pretense and meet each other face
    to face without self-pity and without prejudice.
May we never be hasty in judgment and always generous.
Let us take time for all things; make us to grow calm,
    serene, gentle.

Teach us to put into action our better impulses, straight-
forward, and unafraid.

Grant that we may realize it is the little things that create
difference, that in the big things of life we are at one.

And may we strive to touch and to know the great, common human heart of us all, and, oh Lord God, let
us not to forget to be kind!

— *Mary Stewart*

Seaweed Fountain, Beatrice Fenton. Courtesy of
Brookgreen Gardens.

Take time to play. It is the secret of perpetual
youth. . . .

— *Irish Prayer*

Take the time to work,
It is the price of success.
Take time to think,
It is the source of power.
Take time to play,
It is the secret of perpetual youth.
Take time to read,
It is the fountain of wisdom.
Take time to be friendly,
It is the road to happiness.
Take time to love and to be loved,
It is the privilege of the gods.
Take time to share,
Life is too short to be selfish.
Take time to laugh,
Laughter is the music of the soul.

— *Irish Prayer*

Forgotten Isle

If I could find a land somewhere
That's called Forgotten Isle—
A land that never knew a tear,
But always fed a smile.
A land where Lethe's waters flow,
And slanderers' tongues are still;
Where great and small, and high and low
All strive to do His will.
A land where there is no regret;
A place to start anew.
A land where laws are still unknown,
No treasures locked and barred;
Where seeds of sin were never sown
That have our names so marred—
A land where ne'er a man would sin,

Where all disdain the wrong;
Where strong will help the weak to win,
And weak will help the strong.
I'd like to live in that dear land,
And have my friends with me.
But that on earth was not His plan,
And thus shall never be.

— R.B. Phillips

The Stewardship Of Time

Life is short. Sometimes we are jerked to attention by the brevity of our days and the pressures of life, and death bears in. The words of the Psalmist should become our daily prayer: "So teach us to number our days that we may apply our hearts unto wisdom."

— James Potter

Happiness is not what you have in your pocket but what you have in your heart. Money won't buy happiness. Those who chase happiness rarely catch up to it. Multimillionaire Jay Gould said before he died: "I suppose I am the most miserable man on earth." Happiness lies not in pleasure. Lord Byron, after a life of pleasure, moaned: "The worm, the canker, and grief are mine alone." Power won't produce happiness. Alexander the Great conquered the known world and wept and said: "There are no more worlds to conquer." Happiness lies not in believing "God is dead." Voltaire believed that, and wrote: "I wish I had never been born."

Happiness is being born again. Happiness is in Christ. He said: "Your heart shall rejoice, and your joy no man taketh from you." As Proverbs 16:20 teaches: "Who so trusteth in the Lord, happy is he."

Happiness is being a sovereign individual. Learn to sing solo. Anybody can sing when everybody is singing.

The great and good things of history were performed by individuals, not the mass. Happiness is inequality.

Happiness is opportunity. But there is no more opportunity, you say? Somebody has estimated that 80% of the world's knowledge has been developed in the past 10 years and is doubling every 10 years. Ninety percent of all drugs being prescribed by physicians today were not even known 10 years ago. And 10 years from now, 75% of all people who will work in industry will be producing products that have not yet been invented or discovered.

You're unhappy because you have physical defects, you're not smart, don't express yourself well? Beethoven was deaf. Edison was a poor student. Churchill lisped as a boy.

When Queen Victoria exclaimed to the great pianist, Paderewski: "Ah, you are a genius!" He replied, "Perhaps Your Majesty—but before I was a genius, I was a drudge." There are few born geniuses. Genius is composed mainly of sweat, determination, and courage. If you want success, do sweat it.

"Be sure you're right, then go ahead; be sure you're wrong before you quit." Don't brood over failures; if you must cry over spilt milk, condense it. And don't blame your "bad luck." Luck is a circumstance as rare as an honest politician. Your "luck" is what you make it. Those who complain about the way the ball bounces are invariably the ones who fumbled it.

Happiness is security, and the only real security you'll ever have will come from inside you. You are not the same as the others. You are different. Different from any person alive, or who ever lived, or who ever will live. You are you. The only you. What are you going to do about you? That is up to you. Happiness is a round peg in a round hole.

Happiness is not to ride now, pay later, as the ads say. In the olden days men used to ride chargers, now they marry them. Happiness is riding a charger, not marrying one.

To know others, know yourself. To like others, like yourself. To be honest with others, be honest with yourself. People who continually complain that people don't understand them probably don't understand themselves.

Nobody can cheat you as badly as you cheat yourself. Nobody can defeat you as badly as you can defeat yourself. More important than your good qualities is what you make of them. Happiness is a service above self.

When a young minister asked his Bishop, "What shall I preach about?" the Bishop answered: "Preach about God and preach about 20 minutes."

Happiness is knowing how to spend your time. At your age it's hard for you to appreciate the tyranny of time—there's so little time for each of us. Seneca observed centuries ago: "We are always complaining that our days are few, and then acting as though there would be no end to them."

Jesus had only 33 years on earth. Nathan Hale had -22. Joan of Arc had only 19. It's not how much time you have; it's what you do with it.

Happiness is doing nothing you have to hide. Happiness is a clear conscience. Sin is not old-fashioned; sin is real.

What is mortality? It's what the Bible says it is. Not what some left wing, over-educated professor or a "modernist" preacher may claim.

A nice girl is still one who whispers sweet nothing-doings into her date's ear. Don't ever let anybody sell you the lie that chastity is out of date. Your children will want their mother to be as pure as you want your mother to be. Happiness is having a future, not a past.

All that is legal or "acceptable" is not moral. Only the moral deserve to be free. Freedom and morality are indivisible.

Happiness is knowing. Education is not merely

school. Your education is the continuous development of mind, heart, and character. Character is like an iceberg; the part which counts for most is below the surface. When you cash in your chips for this life, the only thing of any value which you can take with you is your character. Character is a victory, not a gift. Character knows no race, creed, color, or circumstance. If you lack it, it's nobody's fault but your own. Happiness is character.

Happiness is freedom. What is freedom? It is freedom to choose. It is the right of every person to own and

Frog Baby, Edith Barretto Parsons. Courtesy of Brookgreen Gardens.
To laugh often and much. . .
— *Ralph Waldo Emerson*

control his own property, his own mind, and his own labor—as long as he is not infringing on the same rights of others.

There's is only one great giver and that is God, not government. Government don't give freedom; they take freedom. People have to wrest freedom from governments. Then, after the people secure freedom they have to work constantly to keep it. You can't have freedom and security. Happiness lies not in the state but in the state of mind.

Government can give you nothing which it does not first take from somebody else. If you want government to be your servant instead of your master, you must understand it, participate in it, distrust it, and control it. The bigger it is the littler you are.

Happiness is being self-sufficient.

Your parents should do nothing for you which you can do for yourself. Government should do nothing which private interests can do as well or better. And the Federal Government should do nothing which can be done as well or better by local and state governments—and that includes practically everything. The bigger the government is the further removed from the people it is, the more crooked, wasteful, inefficient.. . .

A little boy sitting on a bus between two women unconsciously rubbed his muddy shoes on the white linen dress of the woman on his left.

"Please!" she exclaimed to the woman on his right, "will you have your son keep his dirty feet off me!"

"He is not my boy," the woman replied. "I've never seen him before."

"I'm very sorry!" said the anguished lad, whose feet couldn't even reach the floor, "I didn't mean to!"

"Are you going uptown alone?" he was asked.

"Yes, ma'am," he replied, "I always go alone. My mama and daddy are dead. I live with Aunt Barbara, but she says Aunt Mary ought to do something for me too. So I'm going to Aunt Mary's. I hope she is home, because it's raining and I'll get cold sitting on the steps waiting for her to come home."

"But you are such a little boy to be thrown on your own in a big city!"

"Oh, I get along all right, but I get lonesome sometimes and then when I see anybody I think I'd like to belong to, I sort of nestle up close to her, so I can make believe she's my mother. I was playing like I belonged to that lady. I forgot to keep my feet still. That's why I got her dress dirty."

Throughout our lives one of our greatest needs is to feel wanted and appreciated. No less pitiful than the unwanted boy on the bus are the unwanted old people relegated to rest homes where they get their hearts desire except the one thing they most want: love. Love is the greatest thing there is. Love, honor, and obey your God and your parents. "For God so loved the world, that He gave His only begotten Son, that whosoever believeth in Him should not perish, but have everlasting life."

Happiness is Love.

— *Tom Anderson, (Southern Farm Publication)*

There are nine requisites for contented living:

Health enough to make work a pleasure.

Wealth enough to support your needs.

Strength enough to battle with difficulties and overcome them.

Grace enough to confess your sins and forsake them.

Patience enough to toil until some good is accomplished.

Charity enough to see some good in your neighbor.

Love enough to move you to be useful and helpful to others.

Faith enough to make real the things of God.

Hope enough to remove all anxious fears concerning the future.   — *Author unknown*

Dawn, Unknown artist.

Morning is when I am awake and there is dawn in me.

— *Henry David Thoreau*

L'Apres-Midi Dur Faune, Bryant Baker. Courtesy of Brookgreen Gardens.

> Rise up, my love, my fair one,
> And come away...
> — *Song of Solomon*

LOVE

The Greek language, from which the Bible was translated into English, contains more words, with more exact meanings, than English does. Considerable confusion is therefore created through translation.

In English we have only one word for love; in Greek, there are at least three, each with its specific meaning. One of these words is eros, which refers to passionate or sensual love. Another is phila, which means fondness or affection-faithfulness, to go along-side of one. A third, agapao, pertains to the highest form of love—love of God, love from God, which is self-sacrificial, endless, without expecting love in return.

My beloved spake and said unto me,
Rise up, my love, my fair one, and come away.
For lo, the Winter is past, the rain is over and gone;
The flowers appear on the earth;
The time of singing of birds is come,
And the voice of the turtledove
Is heard in the land.. . .
Come to me, my beloved,
And be like a gazelle or a young stag
    On the mountains of spices.
How beautiful!
Your eyes are those of doves.

Your hair falls across your face like flocks of goats
That frisk across the slopes of Gilead.
Your teeth are white as sheep's wool
    Newly shorn and washed
Perfectly matched, without one missing.
Your lips are like a thread of scarlet—
And how beautiful your mouth.
Your cheeks are matched loveliness behind your locks.
Your neck is stately as the tower of David—
You are so beautiful, my love in every part of you—
You have ravished my heart, my lovely one, my bride;
I am overcome by one glance of your eyes,
By a single bead of your necklace.
How sweet is your love, my darling, my bride.
How much better it is than mere wine.
The perfume of your love is more fragrant
Than all the richest spices.
Your lips, my dear, are made of honey—
My darling bride is like a private garden,
A spring that no one else can have,
    A fountain of my own. . .

O women of Jerusalem, if you find my beloved one,
Tell him that I am sick with love. . . .

My beloved one is tanned and handsome,
Better than ten thousand others!
His head is purest gold and he has wavy, raven hair,
His eyes are like doves beside the water brook, deep and
    quiet.
His cheeks are like sweetly scented beds of spices.
His breath like myrrh. . . .

I am my beloved's and my beloved is mine. . . .

Oh, if only you were my brother; then I could kiss you
    no matter who was watching,
And no one would laugh at me—
For love is strong as death, and
Jealousy is as cruel as the grave.

It flashes fire, the very flame of Jehovah.
Many waters cannot quench the flame of love,
Neither can the floods drown it.
If a man tried to buy it with everything he owned
He couldn't do it.
— from Song of Solomon, (Living Bible)

When She Went Away

The hosts of violets in the vale,
When springtime gives her gentle call,
A million daisies never fail
To pass unnoticed by us all.
The fairest flower I ever knew;
As fair as ever grew in May.
All the while I loved her too,
But never missed her 'til she went away.
— R.B. Phillips

Love is merely a madness, and, I tell you, deserves
so well a dark house and a whip as mad men do; and the
reason why they are not so punished and cured is that
lunacy is so ordinary that the whippers are in love too.
— William Shakespeare, (As You Like It)

Give me my Romeo; and when he shall die,
Take him and cut him out in little stars,
And he will make the face of heaven so fine,
That all the world will be in love with night,
And pay no worship to the garish sun.
— William Shakespeare, (Romeo and Juliet)

—But, soft! What light through yonder window breaks? It is the east, and Juliet is the sun!

—The brightness of her cheek would shame those stars, as day light doth a lamp; her eyes in heaven would through the airy region stream so bright that birds would sing and think it were not night.

— William Shakespeare, (Romeo and Juliet)

And Ruth said [to Naomi], Intreat me not to leave thee, or to return from following after thee: for whither thou goest, I will go; and where thou lodgest, I will lodge: thy people shall be my people, and thy God my God:

Where thou diest, will I die, and there will I be buried: the Lord do so to me, and more also, if ought but death part thee and me.

— Ruth 1:16–17

Pursued, Phimister Proctor. Courtesy of Brookgreen Gardens. Photo: Bobby Phillips.

Perfect love casteth out fear.
— 1 John 4:18

Evangeline
(based on Longfellow's poem)

Back, far back, on Nova Scotia's distant rugged shore
Where forests wail and ocean breakers dash and roar,
Where fishermen of French descent man the surging
      deep,
And herdsmen drive their fleecy flocks o'er plain and
      rocky steep;
Where peasant farmers pick their fruits and harvest
      golden grain.
They fill their modest granaries bursting full and then
      remain
Contented, happy families around the flickering fireside
      dwell,
And many wintry evenings long whereof they'd tell
The sad and fateful story of the almost lost Acadian
      race—
A murky, blackening stain on England's flag she can't
      erase.
A peaceful, lonely nation, scattered far and distance
      wide,
As autumn leaves by winds are spread abroad at
      eventide.
Here young Evangeline, whose heart was true as face
      was fair,
Had lived and breathed the pure and bracing icy air.
'Twas here she met her lover, Gabriel: stalwart, brave
      and strong,
A truer heart than his did ne'er to man belong.
But dragged by force from her to distant lands without
      his own accord.
Her life she spent in search of him; a dying love she
      found as her reward.

— *R.B. Phillips*

Love really has nothing to do with wisdom or experience or logic. It is the prevailing breeze in the land of youth.

— *Lessing*

You Know I Love You

The days are short with you, sweetheart;
They're long when you are away.
My life is only life in part,
When from you night and day

The hand of Love in gentleness
Has touched the tree that never bore.
It gives the saddest heart some bliss,
That never smiled before.

Since you came in I see much more
In bud in tree, in blooming flower;
There's rapture never felt before,
And beauty in each bower.

The red rose tells me of your love;
It blushes for me as you do;
It smiles up at the sun above,
And makes me think of you.

The breezes whisper of you, dear;
The sunshine tells me of you, too;
The birds make music to my ear;
In all I see just you.

Venus herself, the lovely one
Was present at your birth;
She must have touched you with her wand
And placed you here on earth.

You know I love you; I told you so;
I know you love me; you know I know.
Within your heart I know you're true.
Since you love me, and I love you.

— *R.B. Phillips*

He drew a circle that shut me out;
Heretic, rebel, a thing to pout.
But love and I had the wit to win,
We drew a circle that took him in.

— *Edwin Markham*

A little deaf girl on her death bed was assured in sign language that Jesus would come by for her.

"How will He know who you are?" she was asked.

"I'll hold out my empty hand and He'll know me," she confidently replied.

— *R.B. Phillips*

We are so constituted that we must love and be loved to fulfill our natures. We must be needed, and we must feel that our needs are filled in return.

The anguish of loss may be almost unbearable, but still we are forced to forge these bonds of affection, for without them we are incomplete.

The giving of love exposes us to irremediable suffering; but the withholding of love, the wish not to be hurt, cuts us off from the nourishment we need most to realize fully our human selves.

As George MacDonald once put it: "There can be no unity, no delight of love, no harmony, no good in being when there is but one. Two at least are needed for oneness."

It can be husband and wife, friend and friend, parent and child—whatever the combination, we are not one with ourselves as long as we are alone.

— *Sydney Harris*

First Love

This poem was inspired by a painting that depicted Napoleon bidding farewell to his wife, Josephine, upon his decision to marry an Austrian princess to consolidate the empire.

He stood upon the home threshold—
A man of handsome mien;
A mind as bright, a heart as cold,
As ever one has seen.
He holds his hat in readiness;
His look is sad but bold.
From quivering lips he takes a kiss;
His arms, a fainting body hold.

The door is closed and he's away,
A bride of royal blood to wed.
A voice within him seemed to say
Again the things his wife had said:
"Have I not been to you as true
As ever wife could be?
My heart had been each day with you;
It's helped you win each victory

It followed you across the Alps to Spain,
To Egypt, and to Syria, too.
It went with you to Austerlitz and back again.
In e'er reverse, it bled;
In victory, how it did rejoice with you!
Did I not stand beside you to hold your hand
When you did place the kingly crown upon your head?
When millions moved at your astute command,
And blindly walked with you through battles red?

Small pity for you, great Corsican Chief of fame,
Who scorned a love so good, so wondrous, pure,
That you should die on St. Helena's Isle of shame!
What bliss can such ambition e'er insure?
Your heart was surely made of diamond steel,

As hard as e'er your own Damascus blade!
When loved, you dared not let it feel
The joy of love, though destiny forbade."
— *R.B. Phillips*

Love is the only sane and satisfactory solution to the problem of human existence.
— *Eric Fromm*

The Sun Vow, H.A. MacNeill. Courtesy of Brook-green Gardens.

The most beautiful thing in the world is power in the hands of love.
— *Author unknown*

She was a phantom of delight
When first she gleamed upon my sight;
A creature not too bright or good
For human nature's daily food:
For transient sorrows, simple wiles,
Praise, blame, love, kisses, tears, and smiles.
A perfect woman, nobly planned,
To warm, to comfort, and command;
And yet a spirit still, and bright.
With something of angelic light.

— *William Wordsworth*

Beloved, let us love one another: for love is of God; and every one that loveth is born of God, and knoweth God. . . .

God is love; and he that dwelleth in love dwelleth in God, and God in him. . . .

There is no fear in love; but perfect love casteth out fear: because fear hath torment. He that feareth is not made perfect in love.

We love him, because he first loved us.

If a man say, I love God, and hateth his brother, he is a liar. . . .

— *1 John 4:7–20*

Man Cannot Live Without Her

In the beginning when Twashtri came to the creation of woman, he found that he had exhausted his materials in the making of man, and that no solid elements were left. In this dilemma, after profound meditation, he did as follows. He took the rotundity of the moon, and the curves of creepers, and the clinging of tendril and the trembling of grass, and the slenderness of the reed, and the bloom of flowers, and the lightness of leaves, and the tapering of the elephant's trunk, and the glances of deer, and the clustering of rows of bees, and the joyous gaiety of sunbeams, and the weeping of clouds, and the fickleness of the winds, and the timidity of the hare, and the vanity of the peacock, and the softness of the parrot's bosom, and the hardness of adamant, and the sweetness of honey, and the cruelty of the tiger, and the warm glow of fire, and the coldness of snow, and the chattering of jays, and the cooing of the kokila, and the hypocrisy of the crane, and the fidelity of the chakrawaka; and compounding all these together he made woman, and gave her to man. But after one week, man came to him, and said: Lord, this creature that you have given to me makes my life miserable. She chatters incessantly, and teases me beyond endurance, never leaving me alone; and she requires incessant attention, and takes all my time up, and cries about nothing, and is always idle; and so I have come to give her back again, as I cannot live with her. So Twashtri said: Very well: and he took her back. Then after another week, man came again to him, and said: Lord, I find that my life is very lonely since I gave you back that creature. I remember how she used to dance and sing to me; and look at me out of the corner of her eye, and play with me, and cling to me; and her laughter was music, and she was beautiful to look at, and soft to touch: so give her back to me again. So Twashtri said: Very well: and gave her back again. Then after only three days, man came back to him again, and said: Lord, I know now how it is; but after all, I have come to the conclusion that she is more of a trouble than a pleasure to me: so please take her back again. But Twashtri said: Out on you! Be off! I will have no more of this. You must manage how you can. Then man said: But I cannot live with her. And Twashtri replied: Neither could you live without her. And he turned his back on man, and went on with his work. Then man said: What is to be done! For I cannot live either with or without her.

— *F.W. Bain*

In My Garden

Once there were two lovely roses,
In the garden by the way;
Side by side they stood at morning,
And caressed at close of day.
They were always found together,
And their dewdrops they would share;
And it mattered not the weather,
They were always free from care.

As the day broke one spring morning
On the roses in the lawn,
The white rose woke at the sunrise,
And the red rose then was gone.
Ever since upon the petals
There have been for many years
What we mortals would call dewdrops,
But the roses know they're tears.

There's a white rose in the garden,
And a red rose in the lane;
They both still kiss the zephyrs,
And they both still greet the rain;
But they neither are so happy,
And they'll never be again,
Since the one is in the garden,
And the other in the lane.

— R.B. Phillips

When sent down the street on an errand by her
mother, a small girl was late in returning.

"What was the trouble, that you were late?" asked her
anxious mother.

"Well, mother, as I started back home, I saw Mrs.
Smith on her front porch crying," she replied.

"What did you do for Mrs. Smith?"

"I sat down and cried with her," she replied.

— R.B. Phillips

The root of the matter is a very simple, old-fashioned thing, a thing so simple I am almost ashamed to mention it for fear of the derisive smile with which wise cynics will greet my words. The thing I mean—please forgive me for mentioning it—is love, Christian love, or compassion. If you feel this, you have a motive for existence, a guide for action, a reason for courage, an imperative necessity for intellectual honesty.

— Bertrand Russell

I may be able to speak the language of men and even of
    angels,
But if I have not love,
My speech is no more than a noisy gong or a clanging
    bell.
I may have the gift of inspired preaching;
I may have all knowledge and understand all secrets;
I may have all the faith needed to remove mountains—
But if I have not love, I am nothing.

I may give up everything I have,
And even give my body to be burned—
But if I have not love, it does me no good.
Love is patient and kind;
Love is not jealous, or conceited, or proud;
Love is not ill-mannered, or selfish, or irritable;
Love does not keep a record of wrongs.

Love is not happy with evil, but is happy with the truth.
Love never gives up:
Its faith, hope, and patience never fail.
Love is eternal.
There are inspired messages, but they are temporary
   . . .
Meanwhile these three remain: faith, hope, and love;
And the greatest of these is love.

— I Corinthians 13, (English version)

Not only have we perverted the word, we have not practiced it very much.. . .

There were grandparents on an Oklahoma farm who when our parents died took my two brother and me to raise—little stairsteps two, four, and five, they seventy and sixty-five. That is love.

There is a brother who stayed on the farm to work so that I could go off to college, I being the one called to preach and therefore perceived as the more greatly in need of education. That is love.

There is a family which has loved me when I am unlovable, encouraged me when I am discouraged, put up with me when I can't stand myself, and been my most loyal cheering section. That is love.

There are children who honored me even when I neglected them to look after other people's children in the mistaken notion of my indispensability. And now I experience the special serendipity known as grandchildren who love me with unblemished devotion.

I have known the love of a church in dark hours of bottomless grief, in stressful times of misunderstanding, and in joyous moments of shared life. I have been favored with the unmerited affection and trust of students, some of whom do not wait to graduate before coming by to say, "I love you." "I love you" has been echoing through the canyons of my life for a long time. And every echo has its ultimate source in the God who calls out to me in his love.
— *Dr. L.D. Johnson, Furman University Chaplain*

———◆◆◆———

We must break down angers and hates by loving service to everybody. The Christian spirit is irresistible. It melts everything. We gave back the twenty-five million dollar indemnity to China after the Boxer uprising and immediately China's heart melted. You could walk between fighting Chinese armies with an American flag and the fighting would stop. The Christian spirit broke down hates. The only way to overcome evil is with good; the only way to banish darkness is with light.. . .

— E. Stanley Jones

For God so loved the world, that He gave His only begotten Son, that whosoever believeth in him should not perish, but have everlasting life. *— John 3:16*

A Woman

When God made man he did the best he could;
He made the beasts and fishes too,
And said they all were good.
But he said, "I'll make another,
More beautiful and fair;
And love shall be her mother,
And none can e'er compare
For beauty and for grace.
And she shall walk beside the man;
The radiance of her face
Will light him through the land."

A man may do some mighty deeds,
Those deeds that in themselves shall shine.
But, oh, how many hungry souls she feeds,
And adds to little deeds a touch divine.
I ask you, man, to tell me who
Could touch your brow, in fevered pain,
Who can soothe your troubled spirits too,
And make you yearn to live again
    A woman.

— R.B. Phillips

Time and Fates of Man, Paul Manship. Courtesy of Brookgreen
Gardens.

Oh, I have slipped the surly bond of earth. . .
Put out my hand and touched the hand of God.
— *John G. McGee*

IMMORTALITY

*Man not only has a living soul but is a living soul.
Since God made man a living soul, that soul has no
choice but to be eternal. In fact this life here is only a
part of eternal life.*

*I should say to those who don't believe the Holy
Word, "what better do you have to offer that promises
abundant life here and now as well as hereafter?" Where
is the peace and joy we so desire if not in faith in an
all-powerful God and Holy Word?*

*"And the Lord God formed man of the dust of the
ground, and breathed into his nostrils the breath of life;
and man became a living soul."— Genesis 2:7.*

I heard an apocryphal story about a meeting of all
the world's top scientists. It seemed they gathered to con-
struct the ultimate computer, a master brain whose intel-
lect would be able to answer all questions and solve all
mysteries.

In due time the machine was completed and ready
for its first test.

With trembling hands the chief scientist fed in the
query, "How did the world start?" Lights flashed, wheels
whirred, tumblers clicked, the printout began to record
x's and dashes. Then came the ultimate computer's answer—"See Genesis."

— *Robert W. Dickson*

Florence, My Dear

Florence, my dear, I know by faith, just where you are,
Although just now it seems so far
To that celestial, glorious land,
Where God forever holds you in his hand

I still can see your sparkling eyes,
Your vibrant smiles—no longer cries
That here on earth so break our hearts.

Your arms, your legs, your body all
No longer give you pain at all.
I know not how it all shall be,
And glories all that I shall see
When I behold you as you are!

God's wisdom holds from finite man
The glories of that celestial land;
But sometime I will meet with you,
And know you as you are.

— R.B. Phillips

Ode

Our birth is but a sleep and a forgetting;
The soul that rises with us, our life's star,
Hath had elsewhere its setting
And cometh from afar;
Not in entire forgetfulness,
Nor in utter nakedness,
But trailing clouds of glory do we come
From God who is our home.
Heaven lies about us in our infancy!
Shades of prison house begin to close
Upon the growing boy,—
Earth fills her lap with pleasures of her own.
Yearnings she hath in her own natural kind.

— William Wordsworth

Mortal though I be, yea, ephemeral, if but a moment
I gaze up to the night's starry domain of heaven,
Then no longer on earth I stand; I touch the creator,
And my lively spirit drinketh immortality.

— *Ptolemy (Alexandrian astronomer) c. 150 A.D.*

I decline to accept the end of man—I believe that
man will not merely endure; he will prevail. He is immortal, not because he, alone among creatures, has an
inexhaustible voice, but because he has a soul, a spirit
capable of compassion and sacrifice and endurance.

— *William Faulkner*

The Eagle's Egg, Ralph Hamilton Humes. Courtesy of Brookgreen Gardens.

. . . wheeled and soared
and swung high in the sunlit silence.
— *John C. McGee*

The Chambered Nautilus

Build thee more stately mansions, O my soul,
  As the swift seasons roll!
    Leave thy low-vaulted past!
Let each new temple, nobler than the last,
Shut thee from heaven with a dome more vast,
  Till thou at length art free,
Leaving thine outgrown shell by life's unresting sea!
                              — *Oliver Wendell Holmes*

High Flight

Oh, I have slipped the surly bonds of earth,
And danced the skies on laughter silvered wings;
Sunward I've climbed and joined the tumbling mirth
Of sun-split clouds and done a hundred things
You have not dreamed of—wheeled and soared and
      swung
High in the sunlit silence. Hovering there,
I've chased the shouting winds along and flung
My eager craft through footless halls of air.
Up, up the long delirious burning blue
I've topped the windswept heights with easy grace,
Where never lark, or even eagle, flew;
And while, with silent, lifting mind I've trod
The high untrespassed sanctity of space,
Put out my hand and touched the face of God.
                              — *John G. McGee*

Up from the grave He arose,
With a mighty triumph o'er his foes;
He arose a Victor from the dark domain,
And He lives forever with His saints to reign.
He arose! He arose!
Hallelujah! Christ arose!
                              — *Robert Lowery*

Victory, Evelyn B. Longman. Courtesy of Brookgreen Gardens.

He arose! He arose! Hallelujah! Christ arose!
— *Robert Lowery*

About the Author

Robert B. Phillips was born in Mitchell County, North Carolina on October 30, 1902. He was reared within the shadow of Mt. Mitchell, the tallest mountain east of the Mississippi River. His mother died when he was three years old, and he made his home with his grandparents on the farm acquired by them around 1850. As a boy he worked on the farm, cut timber, mined mica, and fired a sawmill boiler. At age twenty he left home to attend high school and then college, both of which he paid for through his own efforts.

After receiving an AB degree from Carson Newman College in Jefferson City, Tennessee, he attended the University of North Carolina. He then served as chairman of a committee to revise the course of study for the state of North Carolina. He then served as a North Carolina high school principal for twenty-three years, including fourteen years at Spruce Pine and two years at Bakersville, and as Mitchell County superintendent of schools for two years. During the time he was principal he taught English and Sociology. After his retirement from school work, he purchased part of his grandfather's old farm, raised beef cattle, and developed one of the first commercial apple orchards in the county.

For fifty years Mr. Phillips made notes and kept a file of legends, stories, and observations current at the time, along with records of the inimitable struggles and joys of his own life. Much of this rich heritage was recorded in his first book, *One of God's Children in Toe River Valley,* which appeared in print in 1983 and attracted significant local and regional attention.

May God bless and keep you through this painful but delightful world.

— R.B. Phillips